WAVES AND MEMORIES

A SHORT STORY COLLECTION

TINA HOGAN GRANT
GORDON GRANT

TINA HOGAN GRANT BOOKS

Edited by Lou Ann Fox, *Fox Paws*, Editor

https://foxpawsediting.com/

Cover Design by T.E. Black Designs

http://www.teblackdesigns.com

❀ Created with Vellum

REVIEWS

"Where do I begin! What a great collection of short stories of Tammy and Dwayne's (Tina Hogan Grant and Gordon) fishing adventures. You are gonna laugh and have oh my moments reading this book. It's definitely a page turner. You have adventures with Sprity, sleepwalking, fires, fog, cold waters, stinky fish, and so much more! Be prepared to just keep reading til the end. Tammy is one heck of a brave girl!." *Karen Wright*

"Waves and Memories will definitely keep you turning the pages. It is a wonderful collection of short stories based on true events." *Darlene Johnson*

"Oh my goodness, the stories of your boating adventures were wonderful. The descriptions made you feel like you were right on the boat with you and Gordon. "*Pam Sheer Vogt*

"There were a couple of times where my stomach clenched and several times I thought Tina was out of her mind. It appears she has no fear. " *Barbara Miller*

"Tina's writing skill brought these short stories to life." *Robin Rennert*

"The authors' stories take us out into the deep waters of the Pacific. They share stories that tell of thrilling, often dangerous times in the open sea.

It truly is a 5-star read." *Debra Kronenberg*

WAVES AND MEMORIES
A Collection of Short Stories
(That didn't make it into the Tammy Mellows Trilogy.)

PREFACE

If you've read the Tammy Mellows Trilogy, then you know it's based on my life and includes many adventures from my commercial fishing days with my husband, Gordon. Tammy Mellow's is based on me, and Dwayne is based on my husband.

Everything in the books happened; only names and places were changed. While writing the trilogy, I wanted to share all of the adventures with you; the good, the challenging and the bad, but if I had done that it would've been a very large trilogy. As hard as it was, I omitted many adventures while making a living and fishing the Pacific Ocean with my husband, but when I asked my readers if they'd like to read about more of our fishing adventures, the response was an overwhelming yes.

I like to keep my readers happy and give them what they want, so I've put together this collection of short stories for you to enjoy. I hope you'll be pleased with more of Tammy's adventures, because my husband Gordon and I certainly had fun reminiscing and writing them.

I would like to give a shoutout to my reading buddies that like to fish. Wouldn't it be fun, ladies, to sit around a campfire and share our stories?

Dana Duplantis, Virgie Lane, Jeanette Johnson, Jacqueline Tibbs, Paula Miller, Veronika Spagnolo, Tina Atkinson, Judy Morris, Pauline Walker, Joyce Carol Mintzas, Renee Dennis Simmons, Darlene Johnson, Marilyn Armstrong Parker, Karen Wright, Vickie Waters.

DUCK! THE HARBOR PATROL IS COMING!

Tammy stepped out of her car in the parking lot of the boatyard and grabbed her overnight bag from the back seat. It would be another fun-filled weekend with her new love interest, Dwayne. No kids, no work, and most of all, no responsibilities. She was here to play, and after her week of waiting tables with irate and rude customers, she was ready to play hard.

She closed her eyes and breathed in the fresh, salty air, enjoying the subtle breeze blowing through her red hair. "One day I hope to call this place home," she said aloud, as she did a 360 twirl with her arms spread like an eagle, heading towards the entrance gate of the boatyard.

Dressed in cut-off Levi shorts, a white tank top and flip-flops, she skipped through the boatyard, waving and smiling at the familiar working crew as she headed toward Dwayne's boat, *The Baywitch*. She was in a fantastic mood and couldn't wait to be wrapped in Dwayne's arms after being apart from him for over a week. He was all she'd thought about, day and night since they'd first met a few months ago, and he'd consumed her thoughts since then.

Before walking down the ramp onto the docks, Tammy stopped and glanced over at *The Baywitch;* she spotted Dwayne immediately on the deck, shirtless, wearing only denim shorts and hosing down the boat. Tammy's heart raced as she admired the view. She couldn't believe how lucky she was to be Dwayne's girl. With dreamy eyes she couldn't help noticing his muscular build, strong arms and blonde hair that rested on his shoulder and glistened in the sun. "He's just so perfect," Tammy whispered under her breath as she headed down the ramp.

When she reached the boat, Dwayne was still hosing down the deck and wasn't aware of her presence. Tammy set her bag on the dock, folded her arms and smiled as she admired Dwayne's backside in his tight Levi shorts. "Hey, sexy!" she hollered, and smiled when Dwayne turned his head.

He matched her smile. "Hey, beautiful. How long have you been standing there?"

"Long enough to admire your sexy butt," she laughed.

Dwayne dropped the hose onto the deck and opened his arms. "Where's my kiss? I've missed you."

Her heart still racing, Tammy skipped into Dwayne's arms. "I've missed you, too," she said, kissing him hard on the lips and stroking his bare chest. "You're all sweaty."

He held her in his arms and smiled. "That's because I've been working hard cleaning the boat for your weekend stay."

"I'm so excited that we get to spend the whole weekend together. Let's spend the entire time in bed," Tammy said, followed by a loud laugh.

Dwayne kissed her again. "That's very tempting, but I have a better idea, well at least for the rest of the day."

Tammy swayed in Dwayne's arms and moistened her lips with her tongue. "Hmm, you do, do you?" as she followed the contours of his chest with her finger, she gazed into his eyes and gave her hair a sexy shake. "So, what do you have in mind?"

"Well, tonight I'm taking you out for dinner to a fancy restaurant, then we're going to come back to the boat, lay on a blanket on the deck and gaze at the stars together, nestled in each other's arms."

"Ooh, I like that. I never get to see the stars in the city. It sounds so romantic." Tammy gave him another flirtatious smile and moistened her lips again. "Maybe a little lovemaking?"

Dwayne lowered his hand to her butt and gave it a gentle squeeze. "Oh, definitely some lovemaking," he replied with a sexy wink.

Dinner was exactly what Dwayne had promised. Romantic, expensive food and a breathtaking view of the Marina from a table out on the patio illuminated by a single candle. Tammy turned and faced Dwayne as they strolled hand-in-hand through the boatyard back to *The Baywitch*. "Thank you for tonight, I had an incredible time."

Dwayne stopped walking, faced her and took her in his arms. "The night's not over yet. It's still early, and look," he said, gazing up at the dark skies, "it's a full moon." He kissed her neck softly and whispered, "now we get to cuddle up on a blanket beneath the stars."

Tammy looked up at the bright moon, "I can't wait. Come on, I'll race you to the boat."

Dwayne laughed as he watched Tammy sprint ahead of him. By the time he'd reached the boat she'd already pulled the cover off the bed and spread it across the deck. "Do you have any beer?" she asked, pulling down her shorts.

Dwayne stepped onto the boat and shook his head. "You know I don't drink. No, I don't have any beer, and besides, I think you had enough over dinner," he laughed, as he watched her throw her shorts at his chest and quickly caught them. "I think you're already a little tipsy."

Tammy spun around, wearing only black lace panties and a

white tank top. "I am, but this is my weekend off." She gave her head a vigorous shake. "I don't get to let loose too often, you know." Tammy glanced around at the other boats. "It's so quiet here. I don't hear anything." She closed her eyes, enjoying the tranquil moment. She looked up at Dwayne and asked, "are we the only ones here?"

Dwayne kicked off his sandals and laid down on the blanket, resting one arm behind his head. "There are a few others that live on their boats, but they're at the other end of the dock." He patted the empty space next to him. "Come lay next to me."

Tammy giggled as she knelt beside him. "Are you going to seduce me?"

"Dressed like that? It'll be hard not to," Dwayne laughed, leaning in and kissing her on the lips.

The kiss was long and sensual, and Tammy melted in his arms instantly. "Is it just me or is it hot?"

Dwayne stroked the side of her cheek as she gazed into his eyes. "It's a warm night, or maybe it's me that's causing you to be hot and bothered," he joked.

Tammy reached for the sky and pulled her top over her head. "I think it's a combination of both. I'm so friggin' hot."

Dwayne's jaw dropped as he watched Tammy pull off her top and throw it over her head. "What are you doing?"

"I'm getting naked. I'm sweating here." She glanced around at the silent docks. "There's no one here."

Dwayne raised his hands in defeat. "Fine, go for it. Do you mind if I watch?"

"Be my guest," she said with a wink, as she slowly slid her panties down her thighs and tossed them aside.

Dwayne remained on the blanket, admiring the view before him of Tammy stark naked and staring at the stillness of the water glistening beneath the bright moon.

Her back was towards him, her arms stretched out. "God, it's so beautiful here. Every time I come down here, all my worries and stress simply disappear. I feel like I'm on vacation, and I can't believe that you get to live here every single day."

"Well, you are on vacation, sort of," Dwayne said, smiling.

Tammy turned around and matched his smile. "You know what I want to do?" Before Dwayne had a chance to ask, she was already on the swimstep of the boat. "I want to go for a swim."

Dwayne sat up in disbelief when water splashed over the back of the boat after Tammy dove in. "Tammy, wait!" he yelled and quickly stood up. "What the hell?" he whispered under his breath. "She's crazy!" Dwayne raced to the stern of the boat, just in time to see Tammy's head pop up to the surface. He laughed loudly which carried across the water. Dwayne waved his arms. "What are you doing? You're nuts," he shouted, laughing and shaking his head, at the same time scanning the harbor for any running boats.

Tammy turned on her back and splashed the water with her hands and laughed again. "This feels fantastic. Come on, jump in," she called.

"You'd better get out of there before a boat comes," Dwayne hollered.

Tammy looked up and down the harbor. "There's no boats anywhere. It's nighttime. Come on! Get naked and come join me for an evening swim beneath the stars."

Dwayne shook his head. "Tammy, the Harbor Patrol boat will be coming by soon," he called in a harsh whisper, but she didn't hear him, and had already flipped her body over and dove under the water. "Shit!" Dwayne said under his breath, scanning the harbor again.

For the next few minutes, Dwayne watched from the stern of the boat as Tammy swam out to the middle of the channel humming a happy tune. Just then he heard the motor off in the distance. "Shit!" He looked at Tammy and waved his arms. "Tammy! The Harbor Patrol is on their way. You have to come back now!" he called out, a sense of urgency in his voice. But she was swimming away from him and couldn't see him waving his arms above his head.

Tammy dove under the water again, feeling exuberated from the chilled water. She flapped her hands and floated around on her back, gazing at the many stars in the sky. "God, this is the life," she said out loud, continuing to kick the water to stay afloat. Then she heard a noise off in the distance and turned on her stomach to look around the harbor. "What's that?" She scanned her surroundings and to her horror, she saw a boat in the middle of the channel heading towards her. "What the hell is a boat doing out here?" She looked across at *The Baywitch* and was shocked to see how far out she'd swum. She didn't have enough time to swim back before the boat would reach her. In a panic, she quickly turned and looked at the park across the way. That, too, was a distance to swim. "Shit! This is not good," Tammy hissed under her breath.

Tammy remained in the middle of the channel treading water, wondering what to do. She no longer felt tipsy. Any aftereffects of her alcohol consumption had quickly disappeared. She wanted nothing more than to be on *The Baywitch* with Dwayne. Again, in a panicked state, she scanned the harbor for options and saw she had none, unless she wanted to be caught swimming naked by the boat that was fast approaching, and for her that was not an option. As it neared where she continued to tread water in the middle of the channel, the water surrounding her was no longer calm and flat. A small wake from the vessel began to stir the waters and Tammy found she had to tread harder to keep afloat. Then she saw the red hull of the boat and the large writing on the side. "Shit, it's the Harbor Patrol. Oh, this is not good." Tammy's heart raced as she pictured herself being pulled onto the boat naked by two sheriffs. "What the hell am I going to do?"

With no more time to waste, Tammy quickly dove under water and remained as still as she could. Her fear now was that she would be sliced into pieces by the propeller of the boat. Holding her breath, she listened to the sound of the motor from beneath the water and struggled to stay under, as the wake in the water increased as the boat cruised by her. Every second dragged on, and she fought to hold her breath beneath the water, but she had no choice. She couldn't let the Sheriffs find her. It would be too embarrassing.

After what seemed like an eternity, and almost out of breath, she noticed the sounds of the motor fading and the wake of the water decreasing. It seemed the boat had passed her. Tammy slowly raised her head just high enough so that her nose and eyes were above water, then immediately gulped in a lungful of air. She glanced down the channel and was delighted to see the stern of the Harbor Patrol boat cruising away in the distance. She lifted her head completely out of the water and sucked in more air. "Damn, that was close." She looked over at *The Baywitch* and saw Dwayne standing on the swimstep waving his arms. "Get back here!" he hollered, knowing the Sheriffs wouldn't hear him over the sound of the motors on their boat.

Tammy waved, "I'm coming!"

When she reached the swimstep, Dwayne laughed as Tammy held out her hand. "What were you thinking?" he said, taking her hand and pulling her out of the water. "You can't be swimming around here naked." He grabbed the towel he'd draped over the rail and wrapped it around Tammy. "If they'd seen you, they would have not only insisted you get on their boat, but they'd probably have given you a ticket."

Tammy's jaw dropped as she stood on the swimstep shivering. "Shit! Why didn't you tell me that? Do you know how embarrassing that would have been?"

Dwayne laughed again, rubbing her shoulders. "Well, you didn't give me a chance. You were in the water and swimming away before I could tell you. That was a damn clever idea ducking under the water, by the way."

"Thanks, but I didn't have a choice. I didn't realize I had swum so far away from the boat." Tammy smacked his chest and cracked a laugh. "Now I know why you didn't jump in. Did you have a good laugh at my expense?" Dwayne pulled her into his arms and embraced her. "I'm not going to lie; I was busting up. There's never a dull moment when you come to visit."

WHERE'D THAT DOG COME FROM?

Tammy was beyond excited when she moved in with Dwayne and became a full-time resident on *The Baywitch*. All of her dreams were coming true. She was with the man of her dreams, living on a boat, with the tranquil Marina as their backyard. But the transition was more of a challenge than she'd expected, especially when it came to cooking meals.

She went from living in a two-bedroom house to six square feet of living space on the boat. *The Baywitch* consisted mainly of a deck to accommodate all of the traps they transported, and the living quarters were minimal. The bed took up the entire v-berth, while the rest of the cabin consisted of a dining nook that seated four, a non-functional bathroom used for storage, and a tiny counter with a small sink.

It hadn't occurred to Tammy when they fished for weeks at a time for lobsters at a remote island, how limited her cooking abilities would be. They lived off cans of tuna fish and cereal bars while fishing and never cooked while out at sea. But when they were home, she craved home cooked meals, and with no oven or stove top, it had become a challenge.

Frustrated with her limited kitchen, Tammy soon invested in a single electric burner and a toaster oven, quickly mastering the tiny oven's capabilities. She could then cook delicious whole chicken, prime rib, beef roast and leg of lamb.

On this day, Tammy was preparing a prime rib dinner with all the fixings. They had just gotten in last night from being out at sea for a week, and Dwayne had left that morning to sell the lobsters and pick up more bait for their next trip out in two days.

With *Prince* songs blasting from the CD player, Tammy sang the lyrics to the songs out loud, moving her body to the beat of the music as she prepared the meat. *"Purple rain. Purple rain,"* she sang at the top of her voice, using a wooden spoon for a microphone. She suddenly stopped when she thought she heard someone call from outside. Tammy pinned her ears and heard a male voice.

"Hello, anyone home?"

Tammy turned around in the small space of the cabin, reached over and turned off the CD player. She then walked up the steps from the cabin onto the deck. She saw no one and called out, "hello?"

She heard the male voice again. "Over here, Tammy."

Tammy followed the sound of the voice to the stern of the boat and looked over the side where she saw Owen, a friend of Dwayne's sitting in a dinghy. She laughed at his Jack Russell, Sprity, who was sitting comfortably on the bow soaking up rays. She'd met Owen a few times and gave him a friendly smile. "Hey Owen, how's it going?"

"It's going good. Is Dwayne around?"

Tammy shook her head. "No, he's not. He won't be back till later this afternoon. You can leave a message on his pager if you'd like. He has it with him."

"Shoot, I was going to ask if he'd watch Sprity for a bit. I have a ton of boats to clean today, and I don't want to leave her on the dinghy all day."

"Why didn't you leave her at home?"

"The little bugger has been getting out of the yard, she almost got herself killed the other day by a car."

Tammy smiled at the dog who stared at her with innocent eyes. "Have you been a bad girl?"

Sprity stood and wagged her tail.

Owen laughed. "Look at that, she likes you. Her normal reaction is to bark at anyone that comes close to the dinghy." Owen hesitated before speaking again and gave Tammy a friendly smile. "Hey, any chance you can watch her?"

Tammy was taken aback by his request. "Oh, I don't know, Owen. It's been years since I've taken care of a dog and we only have a tiny cabin."

"She doesn't take up much space. Look at her, she's tiny, and she's fine running around on the deck. She's great on boats." Owen pleaded with his eyes. "Come on, what do you say? You'll make my dog incredibly happy. It will only be until the sun goes down and I won't be able to clean any more boats."

Tammy stalled as she was answering, wondering how she was going to be able to watch the dog and cook dinner. There was no way to confine the dog in the cabin. But Owen had done an excellent job of putting her on the spot, and she'd feel extremely guilty if she said no. Tammy rolled her eyes. "Okay, I guess."

Owen released a huge smile. "Great! Come onto the swimstep and I'll hand her to you."

"Do you have a pager in case I need to get in touch with you?" Tammy asked, climbing over the back of the boat and onto the swimstep. Sprity immediately stood and wagged her tail profusely.

"I do. After you get Sprity, go grab a pen and paper and I'll give you the number."

Tammy placed her hand in front of Sprity's snout so she could sniff it. "Will she bite me?"

"Not with her tail wagging like that," Owen laughed.

Tammy leaned in and slowly picked up the happy Jack Russell. She was immediately engulfed with wet kisses on her face. "Oh, my goodness! Yes, I'm happy to see you too, little girl," Tammy laughed, trying to pull her face away from the overly excited dog.

"See I told you; she likes you," Owen said with a satisfied grin.

"Do you have any food for her?" Tammy asked.

Owen reached behind him and held up a plastic bag. "I have some treats that should hold her over until I get back."

Tammy leaned over and grabbed the treats with her free hand. "Thanks. Let me put her on the boat and I'll be right back with a pen and paper to write down your pager number."

Owen left a few minutes later after giving Tammy his number, leaving Tammy on the deck with her new friend, Sprity. She looked down at the dog and smiled as Sprity tilted her head to one side and gazed at her with her deep brown eyes. "You're so cute." She scanned the deck. "I don't even have a bed for you." She looked down into the cabin. "Hold on a second," she said. She headed down the steps of the cabin and returned with a pillow and blanket from the bed, placing them by the cabin door. "Here you go."

Sprity sniffed the blanket, then headed down into the cabin and jumped up onto the dinette bench. "Make yourself at home why don't you?" Tammy giggled, petting the top of Sprity's head. "I have to make dinner, so you need to sit there and be a good girl, okay?"

Sprity barked as if she understood, and Tammy laughed before returning to basting the prime rib. Every few minutes she'd look over her shoulder to make sure Sprity was still on the bench. Once the meat was placed in the fridge, Tammy heard the dog jump off the bench and head up the steps to the deck. "Well, Owen was right, you're pretty good on a boat."

Tammy quickly wiped her hands and followed the dog outside, watching as Sprity jumped on the ledge of the boat and then onto the dock. "Hey! Where are you going?" she yelled, quickly leaving the boat to go catch up with her. "Come back here!" she yelled, chasing Sprity, who'd picked up speed and was headed up the ramp to the boatyard. "God damn it!" Tammy hissed, as she sprinted up the ramp and scanned the entire yard. She caught a glimpse of the dog at the exit gate.

Out of breath, she finally reached the gate where Sprity sat patiently, wagging her tail, looking at her with those eyes that melted Tammy's heart. "Oh, I get it. You need to go to the bathroom. Owen must have brought you here before, you certainly know your way around." Tammy opened the gate and Sprity quickly ran over to the nearest patch of grass in the parking lot and did her business.

Tammy praised her, "good girl! Come on, let's go back to the boat." While walking through the boatyard, Tammy's suspicions that Sprity had visited the yard before were confirmed when a few of the workers approached her and petted the dog. "What are you doing with Owen's dog?" one guy asked.

"I'm watching her for a bit."

"She's a little terror, and quick."

Tammy laughed. "She sure is."

Once back on the boat, Tammy checked the time and patted the bench. "Come on, girl. You sit right here. I need to start making dinner, Dwayne will be home soon." But Sprity had her own plans and ignored Tammy's gesture. She walked by Tammy and leapt onto the bed in the v-berth. "Okay, you can sleep there."

Satisfied that Sprity would finally stay put and take a nap, Tammy went to work fixing the prime rib, mashed potatoes, carrots, and gravy. Pleased with no more interruptions from Sprity sleeping soundly on the bed, Tammy was able to finish cooking dinner a few minutes before Dwayne got back.

"Hey, perfect timing! Dinner's ready," she said with a smile as she smoked a cigarette on the deck.

"Great I'm starving," Dwayne replied, standing on the dock. "I'm going to go wash my hands, I'll be right back."

Tammy nodded. "Okay. I'll serve up dinner, it'll be ready when you get back."

Dwayne leaned in and gave her a kiss. "I can't wait, I'm so hungry."

Tammy watched him as he walked up the ramp to the yard's restroom, stubbing out her cigarette in a nearby ashtray and returning to the cabin to serve up dinner.

A few minutes later, Tammy stood back and admired her cooking skills on the two plates, full of delicious food that she'd set on the table. "I swear, I make better meals in a small toaster oven than I ever did when I lived in a house," she said aloud with a grin.

The boat gently rocked when Dwayne stepped on the deck, instantly waking up Sprity. Tammy quickly turned and gave the dog a hard stare. "Ssh, Dwayne doesn't know you're here. Now you be a good girl."

"Oh, that food smells so good!" Dwayne called from the deck. "I can smell it from here."

Tammy climbed the steps up to the deck and met Dwayne in a kiss. "We're having prime rib," she said, gazing into his eyes.

Suddenly they heard a loud crash come from inside the cabin - they both froze. Dwayne's eyes grew wide, "what the hell was that?"

Before Tammy could answer, her jaw dropped when she saw Sprity race across the deck and jump off the boat onto the dock with a prime rib steak grasped in her jaw. "No!" Tammy screamed as she pulled away from Dwayne's arms.

Dwayne furrowed his brow. "Where the hell did that dog come from?"

Tammy watched in horror as the dog continued to run up the ramp and disappear out of sight. "That damn dog!" She looked in the cabin and saw the remains of both meals on the floor amongst shattered dishes. "Damn it! Both meals are ruined," she yelled, stomping her feet.

Dwayne shook his head. "Whose friggin' dog is that, and why is it on our boat?"

Tammy flopped her body into one of the deck chairs. "It's Owen's dog. He came by earlier and asked me to watch her."

"For how long? The damn dog stole our dinner, I was really looking forward to that. I'm so hungry."

Tammy leaned back in the chair in disgust. "He should be here soon."

"Well, he owes us a prime rib dinner," Dwayne said, flopping his body down in the deck chair next to Tammy. "So, what's for dinner now?"

"Pizza." Tammy said, releasing a heavy sigh.

Even though Tammy and Dwayne's first encounter with Sprity didn't get off to a good start, Tammy continued to watch her on occasion and soon grew quite fond of her. She loved Sprity's mischievous manner and spunk, and she'd often keep her company when Dwayne wasn't around. Dwayne on the other hand kept his distance, finding it hard to forgive her for stealing his prime rib dinner.

One afternoon, Dwayne returned to *The Baywitch* and found Sprity sitting on Tammy's lap while she read a book on the deck.

"Oh, I see you're watching the thief again," Dwayne said, stepping onto the boat.

Sprity immediately jumped off Tammy's lap and began barking furiously at Dwayne's feet.

Dwayne jumped back. "Hey! This is my boat, dog!"

Tammy laughed. "She doesn't like you. You two are going to have to call a truce someday."

"It's not me, it's the damn dog. You don't see me barking at her, do you?"

Tammy laughed again. "Hey, can you watch her while I go take a shower?"

Dwayne's jaw dropped. "Your joking, right? She hates me."

"It'll only be for a few minutes; I promise I'll make it quick. Owen came by early this morning and dropped off Sprity, and I've not had a chance to take one."

Dwayne rolled his eyes. "Fine. But if she bites me, it's on you."

Tammy chuckled. "She's not going to bite you." She handed him a plastic bag off the dash. "Here, give her some treats and let her know you're her friend."

"I've tried to be her friend; all she does is growl and bark at me."

Tammy patted his chest and grabbed her shower bag. "I'll be back soon."

Sprity remained on the deck chair, sitting up straight, staring at Dwayne. "It's just you and me, dog," Dwayne said, his eyes narrowed. "Be nice, okay?"

Sprity curled her lip, bared her teeth, and growled before pulling herself up onto her paws.

Dwayne rolled his eyes. "Why don't you like me? You're the one that stole my dinner. I should be mad at you, but here you are, on my boat, growling at me." Dwayne shook his head and chuckled. "I can't believe I'm talking to a dog." He turned to head into the cabin when he noticed a new boat in the slip next to the ramp. It was a 60-foot sailboat; then he noticed a middle-aged man standing on the deck. Dwayne walked to the starboard side of his boat and waved at the new resident. "Howdy."

The man looked across the water and waved back, taking two steaks off the small grill attached to the railing and putting them on a plate which he'd placed on a bench behind him.

"Hey," he called back.

"You're new here. Are you passing through or staying awhile?" Dwayne asked, speaking louder than normal so he could be heard. "My name's Dwayne."

"Nice to meet you, Dwayne. I'm Eddie. My wife and I are spending the night here. We're heading down to Mexico."

"Nice. Beautiful weather for it." A sudden movement of *The*

Baywitch caused Dwayne to turn his head. He gasped when he saw Sprity take a leap off the boat and disappear down the dock. "Oh, shit!" Dwayne whispered under his breath. He quickly turned his head and smiled at the man in the sailboat. "How long have you been sailing?"

"All my life. We try and go sailing as often as we can."

Dwayne nodded. It was then that his jaw dropped when he saw Sprity casually walk up the dock steps and onto the sailboat. What was more surprising was that Eddie was talking in a loud voice about his latest sailing trip and wasn't aware of Sprity's presence. Dwayne struggled to keep a straight face while listening to Eddie's story, at the same time watching Sprity out of the corner of his eye, who had her nose in the air sniffing out the cooling steaks close by.

To refrain from laughing, Dwayne put his hand over his mouth and continued to listen to Eddie and keep the conversation going to distract him from the intruder. Sprity continued to smell the air, then Dwayne saw her eyes zoom in on the two plates. Then, just like a pro and a bolt of lightning, she ran over to the bench, not missing a beat, standing on her hind legs, and grabbed one of the steaks in her jaw.

Dwayne's eyes widened. His jaw dropped, still hidden by his hands as he watched Sprity bolt off the boat and down the dock out of sight. "Oh, no!" Dwayne gasped under his breath, wanting to quickly disappear before Eddie noticed the empty plate. He raised his hand. "Well, Eddie it's been good talking to you. I need to get back to work. Good luck on your voyage tomorrow."

Eddie waved as Dwayne quickly left the crime scene and headed down into the cabin, all the while watching Eddie from the cabin window. Soon Dwayne couldn't control his laughter as he watched Eddie do a double-take at the two plates and pick up the empty one. With a confused look, he scanned the deck of the sailboat and then looked up in the sky. Dwayne assumed he thought that a pelican or a seagull may have stolen his dinner.

Dwayne remained in the cabin, unable to control his laughter until Tammy returned from her shower. "Hey, where's Sprity?" she asked, scanning the deck and cabin of *The Baywitch*.

"Probably in a secluded area of the yard, pigging out on a juicy steak."

Tammy creased her brow. "What?"

Dwayne held his chest, releasing a roaring laugh again and pointed to the sailboat out the window. "That dog stole that guy's steak. Look, he's still looking for it! Now he's looking behind the bench."

"You're kidding! Shit, are you gonna tell him?"

"Hell no, I watched the whole thing while I was talking to him. I could barely keep a straight face. That dog has a serious theft problem," Dwayne laughed.

Over time, Dwayne did eventually grow fond of Sprity, and when they moved into a house a few years later, they adopted Sprity. Because she was such a natural on a boat, she accompanied them on many fishing trips during her 19 wonderful years of life.

IT'S A MONEY FISH!

wayne and Tammy sat on the deck of *The Baywitch* enjoying their morning coffee. It was a glorious morning, the air was still, and the sun was rising over the horizon, reflecting over the waters of the Marina.

Tammy took a sip of her coffee and breathed in the fresh air. "So, what do you want to do this weekend? Matt is spending time with his buddy from school, which means we have the entire weekend to do whatever we want."

Dwayne leaned back in his chair and stretched out his legs. "I don't know," he said with a smirk. "Do you want to go fishing?"

Tammy laughed. "Two fishermen deciding what to do on their free time and they contemplate fishing." She laughed again, "go figure."

"Well, you have to admit, it's perfect conditions for shark fishing. The water's warm, there's no wind, so the ocean will be flat. And besides, we haven't been shark fishing yet this year."

Tammy nodded. "True. I've been craving some fresh mako, too. Is there a lot to do before we're ready?" she asked, tilting her head.

Dwayne shook his head. "Nope, we'll take the *Little Boat*

because it's much cheaper on fuel, and we have bait in the freezer. I have some big reels already rigged with 80-pound test line for the massive fish we just may catch," he said, his eyes bright. "We just need to load the *Little Boat* with food and get fuel on our way out."

Tammy pattered her knees and smiled, "sounds good to me. I've missed being out on the ocean every day since lobster season ended. I can't believe it's been almost three months. Why don't I gather us some food while you grab the bait, and we'll get an early start."

"Sounds good," Dwayne said, taking his last sip of coffee before getting up.

Within the hour they were leaving the fuel dock and heading down the main channel. Tammy took the helm while Dwayne checked the fishing reels and prepared the bait. He held his prize reel with 1,000 yards of 80-pound test and smiled. "I haven't used this baby in a while. If a big fish takes the bait, it should be able to handle it just fine."

Tammy looked over her shoulder and smiled at Dwayne. "Keeping my fingers crossed," she hollered over the loud noise of the outboard.

It had been a while since she'd driven the *Little Boat,* and it felt good to feel the slight breeze blowing through her hair and tickling the back of her neck. Even though it was crab season now, she had not been going out with Dwayne all the time because Matt had school. The salty air filled her sinuses, and the spray from the ocean chilled her skin. "Man, this feels good. We should do this more often."

Dwayne returned the reel he'd been admiring to its holder and joined Tammy at the helm, wrapping his arm around her waist and smiling. "I agree."

She turned her head and grinned before leaning in to give him a kiss. "You never get tired of the ocean, do you? You were just out here two days ago pulling crab traps, and here you are again, fishing for pleasure on your day off."

"Nope. It's where I feel at peace and completely free." Dwayne spun around and opened his arms. "I mean, look at this place." He pointed to the mainland. "Back there is the city, full of chaos and too many rules for *my* liking," he joked. "Ahead of us is nothing but open ocean, no people, and if I want to, I can fish naked."

Tammy tossed back her head and laughed. "Be my guest. Just be careful of any dangling hooks," she chuckled. Scanning the horizon and enjoying seeing the mainland fade off in the distance, she said, "I hear you; this is the place to be."

Ten miles offshore, Dwayne looked at the desolate ocean. "I don't see any boats nearby. Do you want to drop a couple of lines in the water and check out this spot?"

"Sounds good to me, I'll throw some chum in the water," Tammy said, putting the boat in neutral.

Once the lines were in the water and they were drifting, Tammy grabbed two bottles of orange juice and some cereal bars. She handed one to Dwayne. "Here you go, breakfast is served."

"Thanks," Dwayne said, as he took a bottle and a bar and sat them on the deck next to his chair.

Tammy took a seat next to him. "This is so much different than pulling traps. We're constantly doing something at the island, and there's never any time to relax. I think that's why I like it so much. I love to keep busy. Fishing for sharks, we have to sit and wait for a bite. We have so much idle time."

"Yeah, but look where we are. I'd take this idle time over any place."

"You got me on that one." Tammy leaned back in her chair allowing the rays from the sun to warm her face. "I hope we get a mako. We could throw some on the barbecue for tonight's dinner."

"I remember when I first took you shark fishing and I fell asleep, you couldn't wake me up," he laughed. "I was up all night and was dog-tired from getting the boat ready."

"Yes! And the boat was surrounded by sharks. I've never seen such a sight; I had no idea what to do!"

"But we ended up winning the shark tournament that year," Dwayne said proudly.

Tammy matched his proud grin. "We sure did."

Suddenly the beautiful, buzzing sound of a line being taken by a fish startled them. "Fish on!" Dwayne yelled, leaping out of his chair, and grabbing the pole.

"Shit! That didn't take long," Tammy squealed, bolting from her chair. She grabbed the gaff and stood next to Dwayne as he fought the fish. Within ten minutes they had landed a beautiful 80 – 100-pound mako shark on the boat.

"I know what's for dinner tonight," she squealed, helping Dwayne move the shark to the other side of the boat to clean it and put it in the ice chest.

"This is turning out to be a good spot, let's stay here for a while," Dwayne said wiping his hands.

As they sat down to catch their breath, the prize reel suddenly let loose, buzzing loudly as the line was being taken.

"Holy shit! Look at that line go!" Dwayne yelled, grabbing the rod, and hanging on as the line continued to peel off the reel. "Whatever is at the other end of that line is a massive fish, look at all the line it's taking," Dwayne yelled, holding the pole tightly.

"I've never seen anything like it!" Tammy screamed, racing over to Dwayne's side. "Do you need the harness?"

"Maybe. Go grab it off the dash and bring it over." Gripping the pole tightly with both hands, he said, "I need to try and set the hook."

With his many years of experience at fishing, Dwayne was able to set the hook and hold on to the pole as the fish continued to take line. "Shit, he's heading straight for the bottom. What the hell kind of fish is it? He's taken almost half the line."

"I'm going to put the harness on you. There might be one heck of a fight ahead of you." Tammy said, her adrenaline racing.

"Okay, do it quickly," as his chest heaved from the rush he was experiencing.

Tammy quickly wrapped the fighting harness around Dwayne's waist and snapped the buckle. "There you go, it's on."

"Thanks. I need you to steer the boat and stay with the fish at a steady pace. We need to tire him out, and I have a feeling it might be a while before that happens. He's putting up one hell of a fight."

Like Dwayne, Tammy's adrenaline was racing, and her hands shook as she took the wheel.

"Keep it steady," Dwayne hollered as he tried to gain line from the tireless fish. "I wonder what it is?" he shouted, as he managed to reel in a little bit of the line.

Tammy looked over her shoulder while controlling the boat from the helm. "I don't know, but I sure hope it tires soon."

An hour later, Dwayne was slowing gaining line on the fish. "I think he's beginning to get tired. I'm able to reel in some of the line, and I'm getting tired, too," he laughed. We're going to be at Catalina Island soon if I don't bring him in."

Tammy's hand gripped the steering wheel. "Do we have enough gas to go that far?"

"Right now, we're okay. I'm still gaining line, but it's not a lot."

"Just don't lose him," Tammy hollered, slowing down the boat a little more.

Dwayne continued to try and tire out the fish, his hand gripping the pole, his chest heaving. Then suddenly a huge splash startled them, and they saw a huge thresher shark jump at least 50 feet out of the water near the boat, making a perfect arc as it reentered the water.

Dwayne's jaw dropped as he gasped. "Did you see that?"

"I did!" Tammy screamed. "It was huge!"

"It's a money fish! That was a thresher shark; there's no way I'm going to lose this baby, he must be at least 500 pounds."

"We can sell him?" Tammy said, her eyes bright.

Dwayne nodded and smiled. "We sure can if we can ever get

him on the boat. At $2.50 a pound, it's not a bad payday for a day off," he said with an even bigger smile.

Tammy's jaw dropped. "Shit, let's get this baby on the boat!"

Dwayne reeled in more line. "I'm working on it," he chuckled.

After another hour had passed, Tammy and Dwayne switched places, with Tammy taking control of the fishing pole as Dwayne drove the boat. Following strict instructions from Dwayne, she slowly managed to reel in more line for the next hour. "How much friggin' line did this fish take?" Tammy whined, her hands cramping from holding the pole.

"At least two-thirds by the time he went down to the bottom. Let's switch places again. I'm sure your hands and arms are getting tired."

Tammy nodded. "They are, I can't feel my fingers."

Tammy took the wheel and looked ahead. "Shit, we're really close to Catalina. We must be at least 25 miles from the mainland."

"We are, and if we don't get this fish onboard soon, we're going to run out of gas."

"Oh no, that won't be good!" Tammy said, her eyes wide.

"Right! We've been fighting this fish for fifteen miles," Dwayne said as he gained on the line. "I think he's getting tired now, look how much line I'm reeling in. Quick! Put the boat in neutral, grab the gaff and come stand next to me," Dwayne instructed.

Tammy hurriedly followed Dwayne's instructions and peered into the clear water as he continued to gain on the giant fish. "You're getting it!" she screamed. "Keep reeling!" she hollered, jumping up and down with excitement.

Dwayne's chest heaved as he continued to reel in more line. "I'm working on it," he panted.

Tammy leaned over and peered into the water again. "I see it!" Then she gasped. "Oh my god! It's friggin' huge!"

"Get the gaff ready. It's going to take the two of us and all our strength to get it on the boat."

Tammy clutched the gaff tightly, keeping her eyes on the water and watching for the massive thresher shark to be brought to the surface by Dwayne.

"Here it comes!" Dwayne hollered, still gaining line. "Get ready!"

Tammy leaned over the edge of the boat, holding the gaff with two hands. "I'm ready," she yelled, her hands shaking.

Within minutes the giant 500-pound thresher was next to the boat. "Now!" Dwayne hollered.

Tammy reacted instantly and gave the gaff a hard swing. "Got it!" she yelled, her heart racing.

"Perfect spot! Well done!"

The thresher immediately began to bash against the boat, its 8-foot-long tail thrashing from side-to-side, splashing water at them. Tammy shook her head, her hair now drenched and her face wet and salty.

"Don't let go," Dwayne hollered, still hanging on to the reel. "On the count of three, let's try and get this beauty into the boat."

Tammy nodded, "okay."

Dwayne began the countdown. "One, two, three and lift," he screamed as he reached down to grab a second gaff. He then gaffed the thresher in another spot. "Okay, lift again!" he hollered.

Using all their strength, they managed to lift and roll the shark onto the deck of the *Little Boat.* "My god, it's massive!" Tammy squealed, trying to catch her breath. "This has got to be the biggest fish I've ever seen." Tammy looked over at the tail. "Look, it barely fits in the boat, its tail is sticking up in the air."

Dwayne was still trying to catch his breath and nodded. "It's a biggie all right. We may get 800 dollars for this baby after it's dressed out."

Tammy's eyes grew wide. "Really? Wow, not bad for a day off!" She leaned over the edge of the boat to rinse off her hands and saw a huge shadow in the water. "What the hell is that?" she said, pointing.

Dwayne checked to make sure the thresher was secured, then

walked over to where Tammy stood looking into the water. His jaw dropped. "Shit, it's another thresher!"

Tammy looked again and saw the shape of the second thresher. "Oh my god, you're right!"

"Yep. Sometimes they travel in pairs."

"Are we going to try and catch that one too? It's right here, next to the boat. I bet we can."

"I wish. We're almost out of fuel and may not even make it home. What if this fish dives down to the bottom like the first one? We don't have enough fuel to fight it for hours."

"Damn it," Tammy moaned. "That could have been another 800-dollar fish."

"No kidding," Dwayne said, as he walked over to the thresher onboard, checking it one more time. "Okay, let's get out of here. We need to get back to the dock and get this one on ice."

Dwayne was thankful the seas remained calm for their trip back, saving them fuel, a major concern for him. Slowing the boat down to five knots as they entered the main channel of the Marina, he held the wheel tight, knowing they were probably running on fumes. "I hope we make it," he said, looking worried.

"Crossing fingers," Tammy called back, getting the dock lines ready.

Anxious and pleading to the powers that be, they finally pulled into their slip. Tammy quickly jumped off the boat and secured the lines to the cleats. "We made it!" she hollered, feeling relieved.

"Phew. Barely," Dwayne said, turning off the motor.

The size of the thresher and its enormous tail sticking over the stern of the boat soon caught the attention of many people in the boatyard and surrounding docked boats. Within a few minutes they were surrounded by spectators and friends ready to hear about their catch.

Tammy stood next to Dwayne in his arms and smiled at him. "Now, this is fishing," she laughed.

I HATE SHOES

When Tammy moved onto *The Baywitch* with Dwayne, she soon grew fond of going barefoot. When she wasn't fishing, she spent most of her days on the boat or around the dock. When enjoying a delightful book, many times her feet dangled over the side, where she enjoyed the cool, crisp water nipping at her toes.

For Tammy it was too much trouble to keep taking her shoes off and on, every time she had to leave the boat to walk through the yard. She eventually got into the habit of never wearing shoes in the boatyard. She loved the feeling of the warmth of the ground beneath her feet and the comfort being barefoot provided.

Her feet soon toughened up, and whenever she had to wear shoes, her feet felt sweaty and constricted. She couldn't wait to return to the boat, immediately kicking them off.

"Where are your shoes, Tammy?" was a daily question from the boatyard crew whenever she walked through the yard.

And her answer would always be the same. "I hate shoes," she'd reply, laughing as she skipped by.

In the mornings after showering, brushing her teeth and hair,

Tammy frequently walked next door to *Fisherman's Village,* a quaint tourist spot with many shops and restaurants, and bought herself a cup of coffee and a donut. A terrific way to start her day, caffeine, and sugar.

As always, she'd venture there barefoot; after all, it was just next door. On one such morning, she stood at the window of the restaurant that, in her opinion, made the best coffee around. As she was adding sugar and cream to her freshly brewed cup, she heard someone shout, and knew instantly that it was directed at her.

"Hey missy, where are your shoes?"

Tammy turned her head and glanced over at the only occupied table where she saw an older woman with white hair staring at her. The other three, also elderly, had their eyes also focused on her. "Are you talking to me?" Tammy asked.

"Well, you're the only one not wearing shoes, aren't you?" The woman said with an edge, her arms folded.

Tammy looked down at her feet and chuckled, "I guess I am."

"So where are they?" the woman asked again in the same tone.

"I don't like shoes," Tammy replied.

The woman rolled her eyes and grunted. "It doesn't matter if you don't like them, they protect your feet." She rolled her eyes again. "It's not very smart of you not to wear them. Your feet must be covered in cuts, young lady."

Tammy held up a foot and checked her sole, "nope, just dirty," she laughed.

The lady shook her head. "One of these days you're gonna cut your foot up really bad. Walking around barefoot like that is just an accident waiting to happen," the woman snapped.

"I'll take my chances, but thanks for your concern," Tammy replied with a grin.

"What's your name?" The woman asked.

Tammy picked up her coffee and took a sip, "Tammy."

"Do you live around here?"

Tammy nodded. "I live next door on a boat. My boyfriend and I are commercial fisherman."

The woman patted the empty seat next to her at the table. "I'm Greta, and my friends and I meet here every morning. Why don't you join us?"

Tammy hesitated, wondering if Greta would find more faults with her, or maybe it would it be her friends' turn to attack her. "Thanks, but I really need to go."

Greta patted the chair again. "Oh, come on now, we won't bite. Our biting days are over," she laughed along with the others. "We have no teeth left," she joked.

Tammy checked her watch. "Okay then, just for a few minutes."

That few minutes turned into almost two hours. Conversations and laughs were plentiful, and Tammy felt she'd just found four new friends. Each morning since that day, she looked forward to joining the village group for coffee over the next ten years until Greta passed away.

WHEN BAREFOOT DAYS COMES
TO AN END

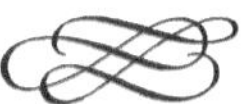

For the first year of living on the boat, Tammy rarely wore shoes. The only exception was when she was building traps in the corner of the boatyard, but even then, she wore only flipflops which was the closest there was to being barefoot. Going barefoot gave her feet flexibility, allowing her to stand on her tiptoes and stretch her body across the wide work bench to cut the wire.

On many days when Matt was in school, she'd work alone building traps while Dwayne fished Malibu, pulling the lobster or crab traps, depending on the season. She'd sing aloud to the tunes blasting from the radio while she cut, bent wire, and clipped the traps together. The next day, she and Dwayne would spend the entire day dipping them in the tar, which prevented them from rusting when dropped at the bottom of the ocean.

After seeing Dwayne off one morning, she stood at the end of the dock and waved, watching him head down the main channel in the *Little Boat* to go pull traps for the day. She'd already dropped Matt off at school and would pick him up at three. That gave her six hours to work on building traps and making bait compartments. She was hoping to get a lot done, hopefully with no distractions.

After she could no longer see Dwayne, she skipped down the dock, grabbing a bottle of orange juice from *The Baywitch* on her way, then headed to the corner of the yard. After turning on the radio and taking a sip of juice, she got to work.

Within an hour she'd built a few traps and had stacked them away from the bench. Pleased with her progress, she decided to cut the wire for the bait compartments. A smaller wire was used, and once she'd loaded the wire onto the roller, she got busy, cutting the wire into the appropriate sizes. As she cut the wire into rectangles, which she would later bend, the unused section was about two inches wide and had needles of wire sticking out and dangling on the ground, still attached to the main roll. Normally Tammy would cut this off before it got too long and became a hazard, but she was so engrossed in her work that she forgot until she stepped backwards and cried in excruciating pain.

"Holy shit, that hurt!" Her foot throbbed from the intense pain, and when she tried to move it, the pain intensified. Tammy looked down. "Oh, shit! This is not good," she cried, her foot throbbing with pain.

She had stepped back onto the unused section of wire still attached to the roll. The two-inch needle of wire had gone through her flipflop and pierced the fleshy underpart of her second toe, coming up through the other side of her toe. Every time she tried to move her foot, the weight from the roll tightened the strain of the dangling wire that was now stuck in her foot. There was no way she could raise her foot to pull out the wire. She was afraid if she did, it might rip off her toe. Every time she tried; the pain was unbearable.

Keeping her foot extremely still so as not to cause any more strain on the wire, Tammy slowly twisted her body at the waist, leaving her leg sticking out away from her body, bracing herself on the work bench with her hands. "Let me think." She closed her eyes and bit her lip to help fight off the continuous pain she was experiencing. "God, this hurts." She looked down at her foot and attempted to lift it again, but suddenly stopped. "Ouch! Shit! I need help." She glanced across the yard and saw that there was no one in sight. She was tucked at the far end away from the rest of the workers. She yelled at the top of her lungs, "Help! Can someone help me?" She waited, but no one came. She yelled again. "Hey! Can someone help me?" Again, no one came. Tammy only heard the power tools as the crew worked on the boats. "No one is going to hear me over all this noise," Tammy hissed. Again, she braced herself on the workbench with her hands, but the pain continued to overwhelm her. Tears pooled in her eyes. "Help!" she screamed again a bit louder, then, to her relief, she saw one of the workers grab an extension cord from the far corner of the yard across from her. "Hey! Can you help me?" she screamed as loud as she could.

The worker suddenly stopped and looked over at Tammy.

Tammy waved her hands frantically, making sure not to move her foot. "I need help! Can you come over here?"

The worker dropped the extension cord and raced over.

Tammy released a heavy sigh of relief when she saw him coming towards her. "Oh, thank god!" When he was closer, she recognized him as a regular part of the crew. "Jose, please help me," she cried.

Jose looked puzzled. "What's the matter?"

"I stepped on some wire and now it's stuck in my foot."

Jose looked down at Tammy's foot and saw the long strand of wire, the needle of wire sticking in her toe and coming out the other side. Dried blood had crusted on the metal and the surrounding skin. Jose's jaw dropped. "Oh, hell no! Can't you just pull it out?" he asked, taking a step back.

Tammy gave her head a hard shake. "No Jose, I can't. When I move my foot, it causes tension on the strand, you can see it's still attached to the roll on the bench. I'm afraid if I try, I'll rip half my toe off. Can you just pull it out please?"

Jose's eyes grew wide, his jaw dropped again. "Me? Hell no! I can't do that."

"Please, Jose. I'm stuck and it really hurts."

"I will go find help. I don't want to hurt you."

"Trust me, nothing can hurt it more than it already does. Please! Just pull the damn thing out!" she begged, straining to keep her leg still.

Jose shook his head. "I can't do that. Let me go find help. I'll be back."

Before she could plead more, Jose left, running through the yard.

"Damn it!" Tammy hissed. "Bloody chicken."

Tammy looked down at her foot and again tried to raise it. "Ouch!" she cried, and immediately gave up. A few minutes later while still bracing the workbench with her hands which were now turning white, Jose returned with two other workers, and Tammy's good friend, Jimmy, a boat owner who was working on his boat in the yard.

"Jimmy! Can you help me?"

The workers stood behind Jimmy as he crouched down and inspected Tammy's foot. "Wow, Tammy! How did you manage to do this?"

"I don't know. I just stepped back, and the wire went straight through my flipflop. I forgot to cut off the excess wire."

"Why the hell are you wearing flipflops around wire? Not the best choice of shoes, you know."

"I know. I hate shoes. Please, I don't need a lecture right now, Jimmy. Can you please just get it out? My foot is killing me."

Jimmy continued to inspect her foot. "Okay, but it's gonna hurt."

"It already hurts. Just do it."

"I'm going to first cut off the strand of wire from the roll to relieve the tension, then I'll be able to pull it out."

Tammy nodded. "Okay."

As soon as Jimmy cut the wire, Tammy felt instant relief, but was still afraid to move her foot.

The workers surrounded Jimmy; their eyes squinted as Jimmy got into position. He turned and looked at Jose and pointed. "Grab that towel off the workbench. It may bleed a lot once the wire is out."

Jose nodded and quickly left the circle, returning with the towel.

Jimmy looked over at Tammy. "Are you ready?"

Tammy nodded, holding tightly onto the bench and closed her eyes. "Just do it."

Jimmy counted, "1, 2, 3," and without hesitating, quickly yanked the wire from her foot.

Tammy screamed. "Holy shit, that friggin' hurts! Oh my god! Do I still have a toe?"

Jimmy grabbed the towel and wrapped her foot to stop the sudden burst of blood, "it's out. You can move your foot now."

Tammy looked down at her wrapped foot, the pain decreasing by the second. "Oh, thank you!"

Jimmy took her hand and steadied her as she hopped over to the nearby plastic chair.

"You good?" Jose asked, as the other workers looked on.

Tammy smiled and nodded. "Yes, thank you for getting me some help."

Jimmy knelt in front of Tammy and unwrapped the towel. "Looks like you're going to be okay. The toe looks fine. Looks like you got a piercing," he laughed, pointing his finger at her, "no more flipflops when cutting wire, okay?"

"Okay, I promise. Thank you."

Word soon spread through the boatyard about Tammy's ordeal, and the next morning when she went into the office, she saw that a new sign had been posted which read – S*hoes MUST be worn in the yard at all times.*

It seemed; Tammy's barefoot days had come to an end.

DON'T ROCK THE DINGHY

Tammy's son Matt soon became well known amongst the community in the Marina once Tammy had moved onto *The Baywitch* with Dwayne. His playground was the boatyard and the waters around the Marina. The crew in the yard grew fond of him, and many times allowed Matt to hang out with them while they worked on the boats.

Games were plentiful and Matt's imagination ran wild - from riding his bike down the docks and into the water with buoys tied to it to prevent it from sinking, to fishing off the docks and collecting whelks and mussels from the rocks. Matt was smart when it came to the water; he'd learned to swim at an early age because of where he lived, so Tammy and Dwayne gave him the freedom to explore.

A favorite adventure of Matt's and his best friend Jake was to spend hours rowing the fiberglass dinghy around the Marina. They'd be gone for hours, checking out the big yachts, teasing and chasing the seals. Some days they'd take a fishing pole and try their luck. They'd often try and race others that were rowing, and most days would dock at Fisherman's Village for an ice cream before returning to *The Baywitch*.

On these excursions, they saw many people they knew; fisherman, the men that worked at the fuel dock, the Marina Sheriffs, the guys at the bait dock, and often they'd see Owen in his dive gear cleaning boat bottoms. Since Tammy adopted his dog Sprity from him, Owen had become a close friend, popping in frequently to visit Sprity. He also liked to joke around with Matt and Jake, and this day was no exception.

Matt and Jake raced through the boatyard after Tammy picked them up from school. Jake was a regular visitor after school since his parents worked. "Can we take the dinghy out?" Matt asked, throwing his backpack on the deck of *The Baywitch*.

Tammy shook her head, staring at the backpack. "Is that where your backpack belongs? Pick it up and put it in the cabin," she ordered.

Matt rolled his eyes, "fine, but can we take the dinghy out? Jake's dad is picking him up in an hour."

"Yes, you can, but don't go too far if Jake has to leave in an hour," Tammy insisted.

"We'll just bob around in the main channel," Matt told her, grabbing two life vests and throwing them in the dinghy tied behind *The Baywitch*. He turned and looked at Jake who was petting Sprity on the dock. "Come on Jake, let's go."

Tammy shook her head and laughed as she watched the two boys climb into the dinghy. "Oh, to have your energy."

Jake grabbed the oars as Matt untied the dinghy and pushed them away from the dock. "Bye, mom," he hollered, waving, and splashing the water with his hands as Jake rowed.

Tammy waved, "bye," and watched as they rowed out to the main channel, then returned to *The Baywitch* where she was making bait jars for the lobster traps.

It was a glorious day, there was no wind and blue skies, a

perfect day for the boys to be on the water. Tammy sat on the deck of *The Baywitch* with Sprity at her feet. She continued making holes in the plastic jars with a heated rod, which allowed the bait to seep through and release a scent. She only had 200 more to do. From where she sat, she could see the boys clearly. They were sitting in the channel, talking boy-talk, and waving at the passing boats.

While looking at the boys, Tammy spotted Owen on the swim-step of a boat docked across from where Matt and Jake were. He was dressed in his dive gear and was removing his mask when he looked in the direction of the boys. He had obviously just finished cleaning the bottom of the boat where he stood. Tammy expected him to get in his dinghy and maybe drive over to Matt and Jake to say hi, but he didn't. Instead, he put his mask back on, dove into the water and began swimming over to the boys.

"What is he doing?" Tammy said aloud, keeping her eyes on Owen. "Why didn't he take his dinghy?"

Tammy continued to watch; the boys had not seen Owen and were oblivious to him swimming towards them. "What are you up to, Owen?" Tammy said to herself with a smirk, shaking her head.

Owen swam out to the channel where the boys had stopped rowing and were now sitting idle in the boat. Suddenly Owen dove under water about 30 feet from the dinghy and disappeared. Tammy didn't take her eyes off the water and waited for Owen to reappear. A few minutes later she burst into laughter, startling Sprity, when she saw the boy's dinghy suddenly being rocked so hard that water splashed over the sides and into the boat. The boy's screams were loud, carrying across the water and reaching Tammy, who continued to laugh. She tried to control her outburst when she saw the two boys grip the sides of the dinghy, holding on for dear life, most likely wondering what was under the boat.

Tammy wiped away her tears of laughter when she realized that Owen had swam under the dinghy and was the one rocking the boat with force. "Oh, my goodness, that's hilarious!" Tammy laughed. Matt and Jake continued to scream as Owen continued to rock the dinghy. After a few minutes of scaring the shit out of the two boys, he rose to the surface of the water and released a roaring laugh, "Hi Matt, hi Jake. Seen any sea monsters lately?"

Matt released his hold on the rail of the dinghy and splashed water in Owen's face. "Man, I thought we were going under," Matt squealed with relief, holding his chest.

"Did I get you?" Owen said with a laugh.

"Yea, you got us. That was mean," Matt barked, before splashing him again.

Jake helped Matt, vigorously splashing water again at Owen, laughing loudly. "Where did you come from?" Jake hollered.

Owen pointed to a boat across the water, where his dinghy was tied up to the swimstep. "Over there. I just finished cleaning the bottom and saw you two. I never waste a golden opportunity to get you two little buggers," he joked.

"We'll get you back," Matt laughed, pointing to *The Baywitch* and waving. "Look, there's my mom, she's laughing too!"

Tammy held her stomach that was now experiencing cramps from laughing so hard and waved at Matt. Tears of laughter continued to stream down her face. "I've never seen anything so funny in my life." She watched as Owen scuffed the boy's hair with his palm and then swim back to his dinghy as the boys rowed back to *The Baywitch*. Tammy met them at the dock and tied off the dinghy. "Are you two, okay?" she said, unable to contain her laughter.

"Did you see what Owen did?" Matt hollered, stepping onto the dock.

Tammy nodded. "I did. That was pretty sneaky of him."

"I'll say," Matt said. "We didn't even see him swimming over to us. He must have been underwater the whole time." He turned and looked at Jake. "Did you see him?"

Jake shook his head. "Nope. I thought we were dead. He almost tipped our boat over!"

"He'd never let anything happen to you," Tammy reminded the boys. "But I would suggest you be on high alert when Owen's nearby. You know how much of a joker he is," Tammy laughed.

YOU'RE ON AN OPEN RADIO CHANNEL, FOOL!

When fishing for lobsters at San Clemente Island, sometimes for seven to ten days straight, life was limited to the confinement of *The Baywitch*. The island is owned by the government and used for Navy Seal training, so no one is allowed to step foot on it.

After a day of fishing and pulling traps, nights were spent anchored in the harbor with limited entertainment. There was no TV reception, and power was limited to a single generator used primarily to charge the battery on the *Little Boat*.

By the end of the day, Tammy's body ached, her hands swollen and chapped, so even holding a book was painful, and reading was certainly out of the question.

What provided the most entertainment and many laughs was the marine radio. It was the only form of communication for all the fisherman in the area to the rest of the world.

Once the sun had gone down, it was replaced with a dark sky illuminated with stars. With the day's catch secured and the decks scrubbed, it was time to get settled in the cabin for the night.

Many of the fisherman would spend that time reaching out to

family and loved ones via the marine radio. It was the busiest time on the radio. But the calls were not private, they were held on an open channel where others could hear everything that was said between both parties: the caller and the receiver. A majority of the fisherman were aware of this and were cautious when speaking, but others it seemed forgot, revealing their secrets to the rest of the fleet.

This night was no exception. After all their chores were done and their bellies full, Tammy and Dwayne curled up on the bed in the v-berth of *The Baywitch* and settled in, engulfed in each other's arms, listening to the voices on the marine radio.

The first two calls were like many they'd heard before; a fisherman calling his wife and kids, telling them about his day and how much he missed them. Another was made to a fisherman's mother, which Tammy thought was sweet.

Then another male voice came on, and just like the previous calls, he asked the marine operator to connect him. After a few rings, the call was connected, and the fisherman spoke. "Hey baby, I'll be at the dock tomorrow around noon. Can you meet me?"

The woman on the other end squealed with excitement, "yes, I'll l be there, I can't wait to see you!"

With her head on Dwayne's chest, Tammy raised up. "Awe, that's so sweet," she whispered. "They must really miss each other. She sounds so excited that he's coming home."

The fisherman spoke again. "I've missed you too, baby. We're going to get it on, so be ready."

The woman giggled. "I'm ready."

"I'll call you when I'm an hour out from the Marina," the fisherman told her.

Tammy chuckled. "Hey, they're going to get it on," she said, nudging Dwayne's arm.

Tammy ceased speaking when she heard the woman again. "I'll be waiting for you," she hollered over the radio.

When the call was ended, the fisherman asked the marine operator to connect him to another number.

Tammy and Dwayne continued to listen and were surprised when another female voice came on the line.

The fisherman said, "hey honey, it's been a slow couple of days. I'm afraid I'm going to have to stay out here for a few more days."

Tammy raised her head higher, her ears piqued.

The woman spoke. "Oh no, I was so looking forward to you coming home."

Tammy's jaw dropped. "That dirty bastard. He's talking to his wife."

He spoke again. "I know honey, me too, but I'll be home in a couple of days, I promise."

"Wow! He lied to his wife so he could go meet his lover. What a jerk!" Tammy hissed.

"No shit," Dwayne laughed. "Doesn't he know he's on an open channel?"

"Obviously not, or he just stupidly forgot," Tammy said, sitting up. "His wife sounds so disappointed. I wish I knew who the guy was. I'd give him a piece of my bloody mind."

Dwayne chuckled. "Well, as we always say, the couple that fishes together, stays together."

Tammy smiled and leaned in, giving Dwayne a warm, tender kiss on the lips. "You've got that right," she smiled again. "I love you."

Dwayne pulled her in. "And I love you."

NOWHERE TO SLEEP

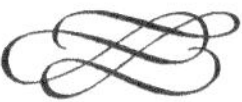

Dwayne and Tammy tried to save money wherever they could, especially when it came to buying supplies for their fishing trips. Between buying fuel, bait, and a week's supply of food, they needed to cut their expenses as much as possible. So, when the fish market told them they had a great deal on skipjack tuna and could give them a great deal on quite a few cases, Dwayne and Tammy jumped on the offer.

"Sure, we'll take 1,000 pounds," Dwayne said enthusiastically. "I've never used skipjack for bait before, you'd better give me my regular order, too, in case the lobsters don't like it."

When they returned to *The Baywitch*, they immediately began stacking the frozen boxes of bait on the deck along with some traps, which they planned to drop off at the island. They had found some good spots and wanted to fish more traps in the area.

An hour later the deck was full, and they still had all the skipjack tuna to load. Tammy looked in the bed of the truck and folded her arms. "Where are we going to put these?"

Dwayne looked at the remaining boxes. "Well, the only place we have left is on the bow."

"We've never stored bait up there before. Will it be okay?"

"Yeah, it should be fine. We'll use it first."

Tammy nodded and pulled one of the boxes toward her and lifted it onto the hand truck. "Sounds good to me."

Dwayne clapped his hands and helped Tammy with the boxes. "Okay then, as soon as the last of the bait is secured on the boat we can get out of here."

The crossing to the island was rougher than usual, with increased swells that broke over the bow for over half the trip. "I didn't think it was going to be this rough out here," Tammy hollered, struggling to step into her slickers to stay dry.

Dwayne stood at the helm, "me neither. The crossing is taking longer than usual because of it. We'll sleep well tonight," he chuckled. "As soon as we're tied up to the mooring, we'll call it a night and get an early start in the morning."

"Sounds good to me. I'm beat," Tammy hollered over the sound of the roaring twin engines and the crashing waves. She looked over her shoulder. "The *Little Boat looks* good. It's still in tow behind us."

"That's a good thing," Dwayne chuckled, looking over his shoulder.

Tammy was relieved to pull into the calm waters of the harbor and be sheltered from the cold winds and relentlessly increasing swells. Even though she was wearing slickers, her body was chilled to the bone and her hair was drenched. "I can't wait to crawl into a warm bed," she said, rubbing her hands together after she'd helped Dwayne secure both boats.

Dwayne scanned the deck of *The Baywitch*. "Everything's still here, it doesn't look like we lost anything on the way over." He stood behind Tammy who was on the deck shivering and rubbed her shoulders. "Come on, let's get you into some dry clothes and into bed. We'll deal with the bait in the morning."

"Sounds good to me, I'm freezing," she said, blowing her warm breath into her hands.

Inside the cabin, Tammy hastily undressed and changed into a nightshirt, anxiously pulling back the covers on the bed. "What is that smell?" she said, creasing her brow and stepping back from the bed. "It stinks over here."

Dwayne chuckled. "It could be anything, we're on a fishing boat, surrounded by other fishing boats."

"Well, it better not keep me awake, I'm so tired. I hope I don't smell it once I drift off into a deep sleep, which I hope will be within the next five minutes."

"Well then, you'd better get into bed. It ain't gonna happen standing up."

Tammy stuck out her tongue. "Ha, ha. Very funny," she replied, and crawled onto the bed. "Oh my god! It's soaking wet in here," she screamed, jumping off the bed and vigorously wiping her hands on her shirt.

Dwayne creased his brow. "What? How can it be wet?"

"I have no idea, but it's soaked." Tammy breathed in heavily through her nose. "And that disgusting smell is from our bed," she shrieked. "What the hell?" she said, placing her hands on the soaked sheet of the bed. "Oh my god, gross! The sheet is covered in slime, and the smell is disgusting."

Dwayne squeezed past Tammy into the tiny cabin. "Let me take a look."

Tammy sat down on the bench of the dinette and watched Dwayne place his palms on the bed. "See? It's soaking wet, and do you smell that stench? We can't sleep in here," Tammy moaned.

"You're right, and where is that smell coming from? Is the bow leaking?" Dwayne questioned.

"Why would it smell if the bow is leaking?"

"I don't know." Dwayne looked up at the ceiling of the v-berth and watched drops of water drip onto the bed. "Oh, no! The bait!"

Tammy was confused. "What about the bait?"

"The bait on the bow, the skipjack tuna, that's what that smell is. It's leaking onto our bed!"

"Oh, you've got to be kidding me, it's supposed to be frozen!"

"Come on, let's go take a look," Dwayne said, heading up the steps.

Tammy rolled her eyes and moaned. "I'm so tired. Where are we going to sleep?" she said, pulling on a pair of sweats.

"We'll figure that out in a minute. I want to go check the bait on the bow."

Tammy's mood had suddenly turned sour. "Hold on. Let me get some shoes on."

Dwayne waited at the top of the cabin stairs and took Tammy's hand as she climbed out of the cabin. She followed him to the bow and stood behind him as he bent down and pressed on one of the boxes.

"Shit, these boxes are like mulch. Everything is defrosted and now leaking through the deck on the bow and onto our bed. Damn it!" he hissed.

"Why is it defrosted already? The other bait on the deck is fine."

"Probably from the swell constantly crossing over the bow. All that water defrosted the bait." He waved his hands in front of his face. "God, it stinks up here. Let's go back on deck."

"Gladly," Tammy said, holding her nose.

"Why would it leak through into the cabin though?" Tammy asked, standing on the deck.

"Because the deck on the bow needs to be refiberglassed, it has some bad spots. I just haven't had time."

Tammy leaned against the captain's chair at the helm and folded her arms. "So, what are we going to do now? We can't sleep in the bed, and we have no way to wash the bedding."

"The only thing I can suggest is what we always do when we want to dry our wet clothes or towels."

"Drape them over the engine of the boat?" Tammy asked.

Dwayne nodded. "Yep. That's all we got. We can drape the sheets and the blankets over the engine. It's still warm and hopefully they'll be dry by morning."

"But they'll still stink of skipjack tuna goo. How disgusting."

"Have any better ideas?" Dwayne asked. "I don't see a laundromat out here," he joked and headed down into the cabin. "I'll strip the bed and hand you the bedding."

Tammy stood at the top of the steps and grabbed the sheets and blankets as Dwayne pulled them off the bed and handed them to her. "Hold your nose," he hollered. "The smell is really bad."

Tammy didn't need to be told twice, and not only did she hold her nose, but kept her mouth tightly shut as she held her breath.

After the bedding had been stripped off, Dwayne joined her on the deck and opened the hatch covering the engines, jumping down next to them. Tammy handed him a piece of bedding one at a time, while Dwayne draped them over the warm engines. "Okay, that was the last one," Tammy said, and then coughed, gagging from the stench that filled the air around them.

Dwayne climbed up onto the deck and closed the hatch. "Now we just have to figure out where to sleep."

"Well, I'm not going to sleep in the cabin. I'll throw up. It smells like rotten fish, and fish goo's soaked all the way through the mattress." She stomped her feet. "This really sucks. I just want to crawl into a warm bed."

Dwayne took her in his arms. "Well, it's not going to happen tonight. Our only option is to dress warm and sleep in the deck chairs."

Tammy pulled away from Dwayne and gave him a hard stare. "What? Out here on the deck?"

"I'm afraid so."

"But it's bloody freezing out here."

"I'm sorry, but we don't have a choice."

"God, we haven't been here five minutes, and already shit's going wrong. I dread to think what the rest of the trip will be like."

Dwayne headed down into the cabin and grabbed his sweater and jacket before tossing Tammy's warm clothes up to her. "I'll leave the cabin door open all night to air it out."

"It's going to need more than airing out. I'm going to scrub the bed with bleach when we get back from fishing tomorrow. That's the only thing that's going to get rid of that foul smell."

After bundling up in their warm clothes, they settled into the deck chairs. Tammy leaned back and looked up at the dark skies, admiring the twinkling of the stars. "Well, at least we have the stars out here. Aren't they gorgeous?"

Dwayne looked up and smiled. "They sure are."

Tammy released a heavy sigh. "What is it about the stars? They always have a soothing effect on me whenever I look at them. No matter how dreadful things may be, the stars always seem to calm me. They're magical in so many ways."

Dwayne took Tammy's hand. "Yes, I agree." He turned his head and looked at her. "Are you warm enough?"

"Yeah, I'll be okay. Let's try and get some sleep, we have a busy day tomorrow."

"You've got that right. Sweet dreams," Dwayne said with a sweet smile.

They didn't have the best night's sleep. Tammy woke up a few times, cold and with a stiff neck, and Dwayne found it impossible to find a comfortable position to sleep in the deck chair. At 4:00 am he was wide awake and gave up, grabbing an orange juice from the ice chest.

The rocking of the boat as he walked across the deck and the sound of the ice chest closing woke Tammy. "Hey, you're awake," she said, sitting up in the chair and placing her hands in her jacket pockets.

"Yeah, I couldn't sleep. Those chairs are not meant for sleeping in. I don't think I slept a wink all night. How about you? Did you get any sleep?"

"I got some, but I got so cold I woke up a lot, and my neck is killing me," she added, rubbing the back of her neck.

"Oh, we'll be in fine shape today," Dwayne laughed, standing up. "I'm going to check the blankets on the engine, then we need to get that stinky bait off the bow and into barrels. We'll get it all off the boat and load it onto the *Little Boat* for today's bait. We'll use it all," he laughed. "I don't want any of that stuff coming back to this boat."

"I agree, and when we get back from pulling traps, I'm going to scrub the hell out of our bed. I'm not sleeping in there until we've gotten rid of the stench."

Dwayne raised the engine hatch, leaning over and getting a blanket off the motor.

"Are they dry?" Tammy asked.

"Yeah, they're dry, but they still stink, and they're all crusty from the goo that dried on them." He held it up. "Look, it's like cardboard."

Tammy curled her lip and hissed. "Damn it. Those are our only blankets. Now what?"

"Well, it looks like we'll be sleeping in our clothes all week, but at least it won't be outside in a deck chair. Thank god we always carry bleach on the boat."

"And when we get back to the mainland, we'll have to fix the bow. There's no way I'm going through this again."

"Oh, that's the last time we store bait on the bow. Never again. It never occurred to me that swells would break over the bow. If we don't have room to stack it on the deck, we're not buying it or bringing it on the boat. New rule," Dwayne laughed.

A SUDDEN CASE OF SLEEPWALKING

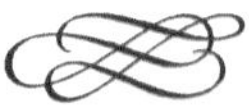

*L*iving on a boat created many concerns for Tammy that she'd never had to deal with before. The most terrifying one was having a five-year-old son living so close to the water. A young boy that never seemed to slow down, was careless at times, and, like most five-year-olds, thought they were immortal.

Tammy would cringe every time Matt raced down the dock, especially when it was wet, fearing he may slip and fall in the water. Even when she yelled, "don't run!" it didn't slow him down. He'd never been around water before and didn't know how to swim. Tammy knew she needed to change that, and fast.

Then one night her fears increased dramatically when Matt began to sleepwalk a few weeks after they'd moved in with Dwayne. Tammy was awakened by footsteps on the dock; she quickly got out of bed and immediately noticed that Matt was not in the cabin.

She spun around in the small cabin, checking every available space, and when her fears were confirmed, she vigorously shook Dwayne out of a deep sleep. "Dwayne! Wake up, Matt's gone!"

Dwayne woke up instantly, "Matt's gone?"

"Yes, he's not here. Get dressed, I'm going to go look for him," Tammy screamed in a panic.

Fearing the worst, Tammy didn't wait for Dwayne and threw on her bathrobe, rushing out of the cabin and onto the dock, where she immediately spotted Matt standing at the end. She yelled, "Matt!" but to her surprise, he didn't respond.

"Something's not right," Tammy whispered loudly as she slowly walked towards him, fearing if she scared him, he may fall into the water. She softened her voice. "Matt, its mommy, can you hear me?" Again, he didn't respond and remained standing still just at the end of the dock, looking straight ahead.

When she was halfway down the dock and closer to Matt, Dwayne joined her. Tammy quickly raised her fingers to her lips to quiet him before he spoke. "I think he's sleepwalking," Tammy whispered. "I heard it can be dangerous to wake them. What do we do?"

Dwayne rested his hands on Tammy shoulders. "We need to guide him back to the boat without startling him," he said, also whispering.

"How?" Tammy hissed.

"He knows your voice, you're his mom. Approach him slowly, persuade him to take your hand, and cautiously lead him back to the boat," Dwayne suggested.

Tammy nodded. "Okay, don't you go anywhere." Tammy held her breath, her heart pounding, taking baby steps toward Matt, her chest heaving and her palms sweaty. She spoke softly. "Matt, can you hear me? It's mommy. It's cold out here, buddy. Do you want to go inside?" she said, tiptoeing down the dock. When she finally reached Matt, she looked at his face. His eyes were closed, and his expression was blank. "My god, he *is* sleepwalking." She carefully reached for his hand and waited to see if he would resist. Much to Tammy's relief, he did not. "Come on Matt, we need to go back to the boat. It's cold, and you aren't wearing any shoes." Matt didn't acknowledge her presence and Tammy gave his hand a little squeeze. "Are you ready?" She gave his arm a gentle tug, and to her surprise, Matt turned around and took a step toward *The Baywitch*. "That's it, buddy, let's get you back into bed."

Tammy didn't rush the process of getting him safely back to the boat, and took small baby steps alongside him, making sure he never let go of her hand. When they reached Dwayne at the other end of the dock, he remained silent, fearing the sound of a different voice may startle him.

When they were alongside their boat, Tammy waited, carefully holding onto Matt's hand as if he were awake. Then Matt stepped onto the deck of the boat with Tammy following closely behind. Tammy exhaled when Matt was safely on the boat, guiding him down into the cabin and under the covers of his bed.

She felt the boat rock when Dwayne stepped on deck, but she remained by Matt's side. Once she was confident, he was okay, she joined Dwayne outside on the deck.

"My god! I can't believe he was sleepwalking. He's never done that before," Tammy said, rubbing her sweaty brow.

Dwayne took her in his arms. "He might be feeling unsettled from the move, it's only been a few weeks. Maybe when he fully adapts to his new surroundings he won't be sleepwalking anymore."

"But how long could it last? I was terrified that he would fall or walk off the dock into the water. He had no idea I was next to him. He didn't even acknowledge me when I called his name. What if we hadn't heard him walking down the dock? He could have fallen into the water and drowned! I'm worried about what may happen in the future." Tammy pulled away from Dwayne's embrace and paced the deck, still rubbing her brow. "We need to figure something out. We live on the water, for god's sake, he can't be sleepwalking around here." She turned and faced Dwayne; her lips tight as she spoke. "I'm signing him up for swimming lessons tomorrow."

"Good idea," Dwayne agreed.

Tammy walked over to Dwayne and wrapped her arms around his waist. As he embraced her, "nothing's going to happen to him, we'll make sure of that," Dwayne told her.

"But what if he sleepwalks again and we don't hear him? That's what scares me."

Dwayne didn't reply right away, trying to come up with a solution to ease Tammy's worries. "I think I have an idea," he said, pulling away from her.

"You do?" Tammy replied, looking perplexed as she watched Dwayne go to the other side of the deck to a tackle box and pull out a reel of fishing line. "Do we have any empty soda cans?" he asked.

"Yes," Tammy said, pointing to the stern. "In that barrel."

"Can you grab me four, and where's the change jar?"

Tammy walked over to the grey barrel and retrieved four soda cans. "The change jar is in the cabin on the floor, behind the steps."

"I'll be right back," he said, disappearing into the cabin.

Tammy had no idea what he was about to muster up and waited for his return. A few minutes later he returned, carrying a paper bowl full of pennies. He then took the cans from Tammy.

"What are you doing?" she asked.

Dwayne took a seat on a deck chair and cut off a long strand of fishing line. "You'll see." He then punctured two small holes in each can and filled each one with some of the coins before tying the cans to the fishing line. When he was finished making his contraption, he stood up.

"I'm going to tie this across the cabin steps at night. If Matt sleepwalks again and goes up the steps, he'll walk into this string of cans, and the coins inside will make a noise, waking us up," he told Tammy, smiling.

"I like that!" Tammy said. "And it may wake up Matt, too."

"That would be good, too. Okay, I'm going to attach it to the steps, then let's try and get some sleep."

A few hours later, Tammy and Dwayne were awakened by the

loud rattle of the coins in the can. Tammy immediately sat up and crawled over Dwayne, lying next to her. She saw Matt at the bottom of the steps, "Matt, are you awake?"

Matt turned his head and gave her a confused look. "Of course, mom. I'm standing up. What is all this stuff on the steps? I need to use the bathroom."

Tammy didn't like the idea of Matt walking on the dock and up the ramp to the bathroom at night alone, and would always leave a bucket on the deck for him to pee in. If he had to go number two, he was instructed to wake her so she could walk with him up to the bathroom.

Tammy sat on the dinette bench and took Matt's hands. "A few hours ago, you were sleepwalking, and I found you walking down the dock."

"What does that mean?" Matt asked.

"It means that while you were sleeping you decided to go for a walk."

Matt looked confused. "I did?"

"Do you remember getting up and walking on the dock?" Dwayne asked from the bed.

Matt turned, looked at him and shook his head.

"Well, you gave us quite a fright buddy, so we hung those Pepsi cans on the steps in case you did it again. I put pennies inside of them so that when you walked into them, they'd make a lot of noise and wake us up, and guess what? It worked!" Dwayne said, smiling. "Look, your mommy and I are awake. It works."

"But I only have to go pee, and I'm already awake."

Tammy laughed. "Yes, but if you sleepwalk again, we now know that we'll hear you and can stop you from walking off the boat. We don't want you falling in the water."

"Why am I walking when I'm asleep?" Matt asked.

"We don't know, honey. But we're going to put these cans here every night until you stop, and tomorrow, I'm signing you up for swimming lessons."

"Okay. Can I go pee now?"

Tammy chuckled. "Yes, go ahead."

Matt climbed up the stairs. Tammy smiled at Dwayne and said, "thank you. Your idea worked really well."

"You're welcome. I just have to remember they're there when *I* have to go pee, "Dwayne chuckled.

HELP, SHARK!

Tammy's love for the ocean was strong whether she was out on a boat fishing, or swimming amongst the waves. Even after spending weeks at a time confined to a boat while fishing for a living, they usually enjoyed what days off they had (which were far and few between) doing something that usually involved the ocean.

One of their favorite pastimes was to take the *Little Boat* out past the shipping lanes, far away from civilization, a couple of fishing poles, and a packed ice chest, then drift in the deep waters casting their poles, eating snacks and sunbathing on the deck, soaking up rays with only the sound of the surrounding water splashing against the hull.

The tranquility and remoteness that the ocean offered was what Tammy and Dwayne craved. These days were few and far between, but it was a time when they were able to appreciate the ocean, take in their surroundings, and not spend the day pulling 300 lobster traps.

Tammy never missed an opportunity to go swimming, so when the conditions were ideal, the water was warm, and the swells were small, she jumped at the chance. Unlike Dwayne, the depth of the water never bothered her. He had spent most of his life on the ocean, knowing what lurks beneath the surface. Swimming in deep waters was something he was not particularly fond of, but instead enjoyed watching Tammy swim from the safety of the boat.

On one such rare event, Tammy and Dwayne had been sunbathing on the deck of the boat for the past hour. The weather was perfect, and the ocean was as flat as a lake. They were spending the day fishing for sharks. Tammy had chummed the water with bloody fish guts to attract the sharks, and now it was time to wait, something Tammy didn't do well - she got bored easily.

"God, I just love it out here," Tammy said, turning over on her stomach. "But I wish the sharks would hurry up and take a bite."

Dwayne laughed. "You have no patience."

Tammy raised her head and looked out over the side of the boat. "There're no other boats out here. I think I'll go for a swim."

Dwayne's jaw dropped, and he quickly sat up. "Are you nuts? We have chum in the water, and it's over 2,000 feet deep out here."

"Since when has that ever stopped me? I'm sweating like crazy; the water will feel good." Tammy gave Dwayne a mischievous grin. "Why don't you join me? It'll be fun."

Dwayne quickly shook his head. "Hell no! I'll be here keeping an eye on the boat."

Tammy laughed and gave him a friendly slap on the chest as she stood up. "One of these days I'll get you to go swimming with me out here."

Dwayne sat up and scanned the area. "You're right. There's not a boat in sight."

Tammy walked over to the side of the boat and stepped up onto the ledge. She turned and smiled. "Are you sure you don't want to come? Last chance."

"Nope, I'm good. I make it a habit not to swim where there's chum in the water."

Tammy raised her arms above her head, and in one swift move, dove into the crisp, cool water. "Oh, this feels fantastic!" she screamed, once her head surfaced above the water.

Dwayne grabbed the Pepsi next to him, took a sip and stood up to watch Tammy. "Don't go too far!" he hollered, shaking his head. "Man, she's crazy," he muttered to himself.

He watched as Tammy swam away from the boat, then hollered again when she was about 75 feet away from the boat. "Okay, that's far enough. You're making me nervous," he said, jokingly.

Tammy laughed aloud. She loved messing with Dwayne, sometimes wondering how he put up with her devious ways. She loved how he wouldn't take his eyes off her, but also understood that to him, he saw her as just a speck in a vast ocean from where he was. She waved at him, and he waved back and smiled. It was then that her mischievous side took over as she screamed and waved her arms frantically shouting, "shark! Shark!"

Dwayne's eyes grew wide as his face turned white. "What? Are you messing with me? That's not funny, Tammy!" he yelled.

Tammy, unable to keep a straight face, laughed hysterically. "I'm sorry, I couldn't resist, you should have seen your face!" She flipped over on her back and took in the brilliant blue sky, enjoying the solitude of the ocean.

Dwayne continued to keep a close eye on her from the boat, smiling when he saw how relaxed and unnerved she was swimming in the deep water. After a few more minutes he hollered, "are you ready to come back yet?"

Tammy turned to face him, treading water as she spoke. "Not really, I'm in heaven out here." She smiled. "In fact, I'm not coming back until you jump in the water."

"What? You're kidding, right?"

"Nope, I'm serious. Jump in the water, then I'll come back to the boat."

"I'm not jumping in the water, Tammy. Have you forgotten that we're fishing for sharks?"

"Then I'm not coming back to the boat," she said with a smirk, splashing her hands and kicking her feet to stay afloat.

"God damn it, quit messing around and come back to the boat."

"Nope. Not until you jump in." Tammy did a roll in the water and laughed. "I'm waiting. I can tread water out here for a long time, Dwayne. You're not going to win this one."

Dwayne shook his head, "damn redhead," he exclaimed. He laughed and checked the surrounding area for any nearby boats or sharks lingering. There were none he could see. "You're seriously going to make me jump in the ocean way out here?"

Tammy splashed the water with her hands. "Yep, you'll love it. Come on, just jump in and I promise I'll come back to the boat."

Dwayne rolled his eyes and chuckled before stepping up on the ledge of the boat. "Okay, fine."

Tammy screamed as he made a huge splash when he entered the water. "Yay!" she hollered, clapping her hands and immediately swimming towards him and into his arms, kissing him hard on the lips. "I told you I'd get you to join me in the water someday," she said with a satisfied smile.

Dwayne splashed water in her face and tickled her side. "That was a dirty trick you played."

"Aaah, but it worked."

Dwayne grabbed the rail of the boat. "Okay, you won, let's get back on the boat. God knows what's swimming beneath us!"

Tammy gave him a salute, "aye aye, captain."

Dwayne gave her a little shove towards the boat. "Oh, now you're listening to me."

Tammy replied, "well, until I want to get my way again," she joked, pulling herself up into the boat.

DWAYNE SAVES THE DAY

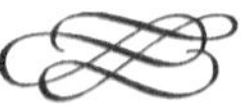

When Tammy quit fishing, Dwayne continued for two more years, and would be gone for up to seven days at a time at San Clemente Island.

Tammy didn't miss the grueling, demanding work or the stress that burdened them, wondering if they'd have a paycheck at the end of the week, but she did miss Dwayne when he was gone and worried about him constantly. It had become a tradition of hers to leave gifts on the boat for him to find. Sometimes she would put chocolates and a sweet note in the ice chest, or a new sweater amongst his clothes; other times it was a gag gift that she knew would make him laugh after a grueling day of fishing. She knew how lonely he must get, sleeping by himself on the boat with no one to talk to, so on one such trip she left him a blow-up doll on her side of the v-berth!

Tammy wished she could have seen his face and heard his laugh when he discovered it tucked under the blankets with its head on the pillow, but the story he told when he returned home was priceless.

On the second day of pulling traps, Todd, a deck hand on

another boat was distraught after his girlfriend called him on the marine radio and ended their relationship. Todd wanted to be anywhere else but stuck on a fishing boat on a remote island for a week, and spent hours on the radio calling sea urchin divers and offering them 100 dollars if they'd come pick him up and give him a ride to the mainland. His efforts failed.

The captain of the boat, Mike, was at his wit's end. Todd stopped being productive, had no desire to work, and moped around the boat in a depressive state.

"I don't know what to do, man," Mike told Dwayne over the radio. "He needs therapy," he joked, and added, "he's a mess."

"What a shitty thing his girlfriend did," Dwayne said. "She breaks up with him, knowing he's stuck out here for a week on a boat. That's pretty cold, don't you think?"

"I'll say, and now I'm stuck with a useless deckhand that thinks his world has come to an end. Not sure how much of this I can take," Mike complained.

"Hang in there, bro," Dwayne told him. "Hopefully he gets over his broken heart by tomorrow."

"I sure as hell hope so. See you out there tomorrow, be safe. I'm out."

After they'd ended the radio call, Dwayne had an idea, and chuckled to himself as he headed into the cabin. Laughing to himself, he grabbed the blow-up doll off the bed. "Oh, this is going to be hilarious!" He removed the packaging from the doll and spent the next 30 minutes blowing it up. "God, this looks bad," Dwayne laughed. "A lonely fisherman on a boat in the middle of nowhere, blowing up a sex doll."

When he was finished with his task, he laughed even harder at the doll when he noticed that she had a hole in her mouth. "Oh jeez, that's hysterical." He had another crazy idea and reached for a black marker on the shelf. He then drew a speech bubble on the doll's face near the mouth and wrote "Oh Todd!" Dwayne held it out and laughed heartily. "I can't wait to see their faces."

The next morning, Dwayne left the harbor before the rest of the boats and went on a search for one of Mike's buoys. When he spotted one, he scanned the area, saw there were no other boats nearby, and worked quickly to pull it up onto his boat. He had to work fast so as not to get busted by the other fishermen. He quickly grabbed the blow-up doll and tied it to the buoy of Mike's trap, then immediately tossed the line back into the water.

Dwayne cracked up, laughing as he watched the trap sink beneath the surface and down to the bottom, leaving the buoy and doll floating on her back, with her legs spread apart on the surface. "Oh my god, that's perfect," Dwayne roared, as he put his boat in gear and sped off.

From a distance where he could still see everything, Dwayne turned off the boat, grabbed his binoculars and waited. Fifteen minutes later he spotted Mike's boat leaving the harbor and waited in anticipation for him to pull up to the trap he'd just left a gift on. "Oh, this should be good," Dwayne chuckled, looking through the binoculars.

Dwayne watched as they approached the trap and laughed at their body language. He could only imagine what they were saying. Mike paused before putting the rope into the puller, scanning the ocean around him and leaning far over the rail to inspect the buoy attached to the rope. As he pulled up the trap and the blow-up doll got closer to the boat, Mike bent over, holding his stomach. Dwayne assumed it was from laughing so much, and then saw Mike wave Todd over to the puller. Todd leaned over the rail, inspected the incoming trap, and then did some mysterious body moves, consisting of hops and jumps on the deck before bringing the trap onto the boat.

Dwayne put down the binoculars and wiped the tears from his eyes. He could no longer see between tears from laughing so much and heard Mike calling him over the radio.

"Hey, Dwayne. You got me?"

Dwayne tried to control his continuous laughter before getting on the radio. "Yeah, I got you, Mike."

"Todd got a gift on our first trap. You didn't happen to have anything to do with that did you?"

Dwayne was still laughing and released a loud cough as he wiped more tears away from his eyes. "Well, that depends. Does he like it?"

"He's busting up man, and dancing with her on the deck. I think he's doing the tango. You should see this, it's friggin' hilarious! I think he's in love."

"That's good to hear, I thought he could use a bit of cheering up after what his girlfriend did to him yesterday."

"I've never seen him so happy, not even with his ex-girlfriend," Mike joked. "I think you may have saved the day, thanks man."

"Hey, he needed to be snapped out of the rabbit hole he was heading down. I'll catch up with you later and see how he's doing. Have a great day, I'm out."

Later in the day, halfway down his line of traps, Dwayne spotted Mike's boat and slowed down to say howdy. But it wasn't Mike or Todd that caught his attention first, it was the doll, dressed in slickers, gloves and a baseball hat, tied to the mast. "I see you have a new crew member," Dwayne laughed.

Todd looked at the doll, "her name's Polly. She's our mascot, and she keeps an eye out for annoying seagulls."

"Looks like you're doing better, Todd," Dwayne said, trying to keep a straight face.

"Couldn't be better. Thanks man, I needed a good laugh. I like Polly, she doesn't talk back," Todd joked.

"Any time, I'll see you guys back in the Marina." Dwayne waved at the doll. "Bye Polly," and chuckled to himself as he put the boat in gear and sped off.

Back at the harbor, exhausted from pulling traps all day, Dwayne spent the early evening prepping bait for tomorrow's pull and then settled into the cabin with a cup of hot chocolate and a can of Dinty Moore's beef stew. An hour later he heard Mike calling him on the radio. "Dwayne, you got me?"

Dwayne crawled off the bed and headed up the stairs to the helm where the radio was mounted on the dash. "Yeah, I gotcha. How's lover boy doing?"

Mike laughed. "He's in heaven, man. He had a bit to drink tonight and is now curled up in bed with Polly."

"What? He took the doll to bed with him?" Dwayne laughed.

"He sure did. I'm telling you, he's in love. But seriously man, I wanted to call and thank you for saving not only the day, but the whole dang trip. He was so depressed, I honestly thought he was going to abandon ship, so thanks. That was the best prank ever."

"Don't thank me, thank Polly," Dwayne chuckled.

FIRE!

It was payday for Tammy and Dwayne. After spending a week at sea working round the clock, it was time to cash in on their lobster catch and reap the rewards. Even though they were exhausted from their nine-hour crossing back to the mainland, they never wasted any time selling the lobsters.

Because buyers only bought live lobsters, they were up at the crack of dawn when the markets were open and hustled to get them sold. Keeping them alive was intense, and every lobster that died was money down the drain.

"Who's buying this load?" Tammy asked, helping Dwayne load the lobster receivers into the truck.

"The seafood restaurant in Malibu."

"Oh, goodie. Do we have time to have lunch there? They have the best fish and chips."

Dwayne smiled. "Sure, we're not heading back to the island for two more days. We've worked hard and deserve a delicious meal before we live off cans of tuna fish and granola bars at the island for a week," he laughed.

After the truck was loaded, Dwayne used the payphone to call the owner of the restaurant and let him know they were on their way. Tammy stayed at the truck and covered the lobster receivers with towels that had been soaked in ocean water, keeping the lobsters cool and moist. She then chased down Sprity, their Jack Russell terrier, put her in the cab of the truck and waited for Dwayne to return.

It was about an hour drive to Malibu from the Marina, and Tammy turned on the radio once they were on the road. "Do you want to listen to music or the news?" she asked.

"Leave the news on. I want to hear the weather."

Tammy leaned back in her seat and was about to doze off when a news story caught her attention. "Shit! Did you hear that? There's a fire in Malibu."

"I did. Let's hope it's not near the restaurant. These lobsters will never survive an hour trip back to the Marina."

"Oh god, I hope not! We could lose our entire catch. A week's worth of hard labor would be completely gone down the drain. We'd be screwed," Tammy said worriedly.

Dwayne sighed and nodded, "yeah, we would be. Part of this money is paying for our next trip out to the island."

"Did Pete, the owner of the restaurant mention anything about the fire?"

"No, he didn't, I guess he's not in any danger."

"Well, that's a relief, sounds like we'll be okay."

Feeling relieved, Tammy leaned back in her seat and closed her eyes. She was exhausted from no sleep, and even though she'd tried to take a nap on the boat during the crossing home, she'd never been able to sleep on the boat when it was moving. The roaring noise of the engine, the crashing of the waves against the hull, and the constant rocking motion of the boat made it impossible.

She managed to doze off for half of the journey to Malibu but was rudely awakened by Sprity jumping on her lap and licking her face. "Jesus, dog, you scared the crap out of me," Tammy shrieked, wiping her face.

Dwayne laughed, "you were snoring over there, I think you were keeping Sprity awake!"

Tammy sat up. "No, I wasn't," she protested, placing Sprity on the seat between them before looking out the window. "See any smoke from the fire?"

"No, and I've been looking. Must be back in the hills somewhere. I think we'll be okay."

When they arrived at the restaurant, they immediately found Pete and began unloading the lobsters into his tanks. Once they were out of the receivers and in Pete's tanks, they were now his responsibility.

"Do you two want some lunch?" Pete asked Dwayne, handing him a check. "It's on the house."

Tammy quickly answered. "We would love it. Thanks, I'm starving."

Dwayne leaned against the truck and looked up at the hills behind the restaurant. "I see smoke up there. Have you heard any more on the fire?" he asked Pete.

"It's about a mile away, I'm not too worried. Every time we have a fire out here, this parking lot fills up with fire trucks. I expect to see them pulling in any minute."

Dwayne looked around at the accumulating smoke building up in the sky. "Don't you think you should fill some barrels up with water? Look at this place, you're surrounded by hillsides covered with brush on all sides that haven't seen rain in months. Fires move pretty fast, and if it's just behind that ridge, you may want to be prepared," Dwayne advised Pete. "I also heard on the radio driving up here that the fire department has a new policy in place this year. It's completely different from previous years."

"They do? What's that?" Pete asked concernedly.

"They no longer have a group of fire trucks in one place now.

One truck is assigned to a structure that may be at risk. So, more than likely, all the fire trucks handling this fire are stationed at various locations, which is why there aren't any here." Dwayne looked up at the hillside, then again at the rest of the hillsides surrounding the restaurant. "That plume is growing and getting really smoky. I think we need to gather up as many barrels and containers as we can find on your property and fill them with water. We'll place them all around the restaurant, and some on the roof. If the fire gets close, we can wet everything down," Dwayne suggested.

Pete looked up at the smoke creeping up behind the ridge and rising into the sky. "Shit! I'll round up as many people as I can. Thanks man, for sticking around."

"No problem, Tammy and I'll start looking for barrels and containers."

"Let me check on Sprity, she's in the truck," Tammy said before racing over to the truck parked under a palm tree. She peered into the window. "She's fine. She's sleeping," she hollered, running back to Dwayne's side. "It's getting really smoky, my eyes are burning," she said, wiping her eyes.

"Come on, start gathering anything that will hold water and pile them up by the hose. The Santa Anas are beginning to pick up. We need to move fast; if that fire crests the top of the ridge, it'll race down that hill," Dwayne said sharply.

"Do you think that'll happen?" Tammy asked.

"Well, we're not going to stand around here and wait to find out. Come on."

Tammy followed Dwayne, and together they searched the property for containers. Others who Pete had spoken with came to assist, asking for their help. Within five minutes the smoke was now thick like Tule fog; people were coughing, covering their mouths with their hands, and wiping their endlessly watering eyes. "God, I can't breathe," Tammy screamed between harsh coughs.

"We need to find some towels or t-shirts, anything we can soak in water, and tie them over our mouths and noses," Dwayne yelled, his hand over his mouth.

"I have a pile of towels in the kitchen," Pete shouted, running to the back door of the restaurant, and returning a few minutes later with a handful of towels.

"Throw them in a bucket of water," Dwayne hollered. He turned to the crowd of volunteers and asked for their help in the search for more containers and stacking them near the hose. "Everyone grab a wet towel from the bucket and tie it around your head so that your mouth and nose are covered. You don't want to be breathing in this heavy smoke."

"The hose has no water pressure!" yelled a guy who'd been assigned to filling buckets and barrels hollered. "It's going to take forever to fill these!"

"I see flames!" Tammy hollered, looking up at the hill.

Pete and Dwayne stared at the ridgeline. "I'll give it five minutes before it crests the top," Dwayne shouted. "We need to move fast!" He turned to the man at the hose, "keep filling those buckets. The rest of us will spread them around the parking lot and put some on the roof."

After grabbing a wet towel, people scurried in a frenzy to all corners of the parking lot and to the patio where wooden tables filled the area, and alongside the restaurant which was completely made of wood, placing buckets and barrels in high-risk areas. Dwayne and Pete climbed onto the roof with the hose and began hosing down the rooftop.

"Look Pete, the flames have crested the top of the ridgeline," Dwayne hollered, pointing.

Pete looked up and hollered, "fuck!"

"Keep soaking the roof," Dwayne shouted, his eyes watering from the smoke that was now so thick that he couldn't see across Pacific Coast Highway. "We need to soak everything around here. I'm going down to tell everyone to pour water on anything that may burn."

When he jumped off the lowest part of the roof, Tammy raced over to him and pointed to the hillside. "Do you see the flames?" she shrieked. They're coming down this side of the hill!"

"Yes, we have to wet down as much as we can with the water we've collected," Dwayne told her.

Tammy looked up at the dark sky, flying embers twisting in the smoke that was now blanketing the entire area around the restaurant. Constant tears pooled in her stinging eyes and ran down her cheeks, and she struggled to see clearly. "Shit, I can't see 40 feet in front of me, and my throat is killing me," she told Dwayne, her voice hoarse.

"Hold your breath as much as you can and change the towel around your face if it gets too dry," Dwayne told her. "I'm going to go over to the patio dining tables and help drench the area with water."

"I'm going to stay close to the restaurant and see how I can help," Tammy hollered, ducking her head from the growing winds and flying embers.

Tammy looked up at the hillside and saw that the flames had grown twice in size and were now roaring down the hillside. "Oh my god, that's not good." She watched in horror as a flying ember landed on top of a palm tree, and within minutes, the palm tree fronds ignited into flames. "Holy shit!"

Tammy scanned the tall palm trees circling the parking lot and screamed. "Oh my god, our truck is parked under a burning palm tree; Sprity's in there!" Tammy gasped when she not only saw the fronds of the tree burst into flames, but also the trunk. Her heart raced as she ran over to the outside sitting area in search of Dwayne. "Dwayne! Dwayne!" she hollered as loud as she could, her voice hoarse, her throat like sandpaper. She finally spotted him in the upper seating area, pouring water over the wooden tables and benches. Out of breath, Tammy finally reached him and held her chest as she tried to catch her breath. "Dwayne, we need to move the truck. It's parked under a burning palm tree and Sprity is in there," she gasped between short, heaving breaths.

Dwayne froze and looked over to where his truck was parked. "Oh, shit! Stay here and keep pouring water on these tables. I'll go move the truck."

"Do we need to get Sprity out of there?"

Dwayne shook his head. "No, she's safer in the truck. I'll park it across the road near the beach."

Tammy used all the water in the buckets and gathered up as many as she could, racing back to the hose to refill them. She noticed a guy that had just finished filling up a barrel with water and said, "I'm going to fill the buckets from this barrel, it'll be much quicker to dunk the buckets in the barrel than use the hose."

The guy waved okay and nodded, saying, "I'll top off the barrel when you're done."

Tammy was working at an accelerated pace when she felt a hand grab the back of her neck and forcefully push her head into the barrel of water until her head was fully submerged. A few seconds later her head was pulled back up. Tammy pulled herself away, coughed hard, and immediately turned around and found herself face-to-face with a man she didn't know. "What the hell are you doing?" she screamed, shaking her soaked hair.

"I'm so sorry, but your hair was on fire!" he yelled.

Tammy's jaw dropped. "It was? Oh shit, I had no idea." Her tone quickly changed. "Thank you for acting so quickly."

"A flying ember must have landed in your hair, but it's out now. I'm sorry, I didn't mean to scare you."

Tammy waved her hand, "no, it's perfectly okay. Thanks for saving my hair."

After he moved the truck, Dwayne joined them. "Everything okay?" he asked, resting his hand on Tammy's shoulder. "Why's your hair all wet?"

"This man saw that my hair was on fire and took immediate

action; he dunked my head in this barrel of water. I owe him a big thank you, I had no idea."

"Oh, wow!" Dwayne turned to him and said, "thanks, man."

"How's Sprity?" Tammy asked with concern.

Dwayne pointed to the truck now parked across the main road. "She's sleeping, oblivious to what's going on. I heard sirens, too. Let's hope firetrucks are making their way here. They seem to be getting closer."

"God, I hope so. I'm not sure how much time we have, or if we need to evacuate. The smoke is becoming unbearable, some people have already left."

"I'm going to go find Pete and hose down the roof some more."

Tammy nodded. "Okay, I'm going to see if I can see any firetrucks and flag them down. We need help."

"Good idea," Dwayne hollered, grabbing the hose, and running toward the restaurant.

Tammy retied the towel around her face that had come loose and ran across the parking lot, out to the main road. She'd never seen Pacific Coast Highway so desolate. She ran out to the middle of the road and looked in either direction. An eerie, dark cloud of smoke drifted over the ocean, and dense smoke blanketed her surroundings lit by thousands of flying embers being thrust in all directions by the intense Santa Anas.

Tammy's vision was limited by the heavy smoke; she coughed to clear her lungs and aid her annoying sore throat. The hillsides were lit up with flashing red lights as firefighters tried to save threatened homes and put out the fires of those already burning. She heard sirens off in the distance, and, like Dwayne, wondering if they would reach them. With her eyes strained and stinging from the smoke, she stared hard down the empty, eerie road, swearing that the noise from the sirens was getting louder. "It sounds like they're getting closer. Please be coming here," Tammy yelled out loudly. Within minutes she saw the red lights of a firetruck racing towards her, breaking through the heavy smoke.

Tammy jumped up and down, waving her arms in a panicked state. "Over here! We need help!" She continued to make noise and wave her arms frantically above her head, then she saw a second firetruck break through the smoke. "Oh god, yes!" she screamed, jumping up and down. "Over here!" she screamed again, pointing to the restaurant.

When the firetrucks slowed down, Tammy moved out of the middle of the road and yelled at one of the firemen who was leaning out of the window. "Please, we need help! The fire is racing down the hillside behind the restaurant. We've been pouring water on everything, but we can hardly breathe because of the smoke."

The fireman nodded and yelled, "we're on it!" as the two trucks drove into the parking lot.

Tammy raced behind them, her heart racing and the adrenaline in high gear. "The firetrucks are here!" she yelled at anyone crossing her path. She had no idea how long they'd been fighting the fire, but relief began to settle in as she watched the firemen, jumping out of the trucks and charging over to the hydrants with their hoses. Within seconds they had gallons of water flooding the area. Just then, Tammy heard a loud roar in the sky and jumped for joy along with the rest of the people, when a red and yellow super scooper plane flew low over the restaurant and dumped fire retardant on the hillside, drenching the hillside and anyone close by. The flames were immediately knocked down and Tammy screamed, "Yes!" as the volunteers roared and cheered loudly.

Dwayne soon joined Tammy as she stood at the entrance to the parking lot, wrapping his arm around her waist. Together they watched the super scooper return twice with two more loads of fire retardant. "What a beautiful sight," Tammy said, shielding her head in Dwayne's chest trying to conceal her face, still wrapped in a damp rag, from the endless plumes of smoke and fire retardant.

"Yeah, it sure is. I think Pete and the restaurant will be okay," Dwayne smiled.

"Yeah, me too," Tammy said.

They both remained out of the way of the firefighters so they could do their job. Some of the volunteers began to leave, unsure if the roads to their homes were open.

"Do you think we should get going?" Tammy asked. "I don't want to get stranded out here. Matt is going home with his friend after school, but we need to pick him up tonight."

"Yeah, let me go talk to Pete and see if he needs any more help, but it looks like they're getting the fire under control," he said, releasing his hold on Tammy. "I'll be right back."

"Give me the keys, I'll wait for you in the truck. I want to check on Sprity."

When Tammy reached the truck, she freed her mouth and nose from the damp rag, unlocked the door and grabbed the leash on the seat. Sprity jumped up, startled by her presence. "Hey, girl, how're you doing?" She hooked her collar to the leash and picked her up. "Come on, I'm sure you need to go potty."

The main road was still desolate, and Tammy feared it may be closed a few miles away. "Shit, I hope we can get out of here."

A few minutes later after putting Sprity back in the cab of the truck, she spotted Dwayne crossing the empty highway and walking towards them. He had removed the towel from his face, and his smile soothed her.

"How's Pete doing?" Tammy asked, stepping into the truck.

"He's doing much better than he was a few hours ago and was very appreciative of our help. He said that lunch is on him, any time," he laughed. "He said the restaurant will be fine, and insisted we leave before we get stuck here."

"I was thinking the same thing. Look at this road, it's empty. I hope it's not closed further down."

Dwayne fired up the truck and petted the top of Sprity's head. "Come on, let's get out of here."

For a few miles, the road was wide open. "This is so eerie," Tammy said, looking out the window. "I've never seen this road with no cars on it before. And look at the smoke, it's much thicker here."

Dwayne pointed out the windshield. "Yeah, I can barely see, and I'm only going about ten miles an hour." His tone suddenly changed, "Shit, look up ahead, I see brake lights."

"Oh crap. Have they closed the road?"

When they were finally able to make out all the cars, they saw they were being led into the Michael Landon Center on the right. Dwayne came to a complete stop behind the mass of cars. A few minutes later a man wearing a mask approached their truck. Tammy rolled down her window. "What's going on?" she asked.

"The road is closed three miles up ahead, and everyone is being directed to the evacuation center, the Michael Landon Center."

"Shit," Tammy hissed.

Dwayne leaned over and said, "how long will the road be closed?"

"We have no idea, sir. Please pull into the parking lot and remain in your truck for further instructions. The building is full."

Dwayne nodded. "Will do, thanks."

Rolling up her window, Tammy waved at the man as Dwayne followed the other cars into the parking area and found a place off to the left near some grass.

"I wonder how long we're going to be stuck here?"

Dwayne leaned back in his seat. "Who knows. It must be pretty bad to close the main highway into Santa Monica."

"This is not good." Tammy glanced at her watch. "It's almost four o'clock. Matt will be at his friend's house, and I have no way to call." Tammy looked out of the window. I can't believe this friggin' smoke, and look up there, I see a house totally engulfed in flames." Tammy's adrenaline began to rise again, "that fire could spread all the way down here and jump the highway."

"Look at all the flying embers around us," Dwayne said, scanning the parking lot. He looked over at the building and the other cars. "Wait! People are running out of the building and racing to their cars. Some cars are leaving. What the hell is going on?"

Tammy strained her eyes to look through the smoke. "Why are they leaving?"

Dwayne wound down his window and called to a man racing to his car." Hey! What's going on?"

The man, no more than ten feet from the truck, covered his mouth with his sleeve. "They're evacuating the Center. They've set up another one a few miles down the road."

"Fuck!" Dwayne yelled, firing up the truck. "I see a staff member over there, waving cars to the exit. I'm going to go talk to him."

Tammy pet Sprity, who'd jumped onto her lap as they drove slowly towards the exit. When they reached the man, Dwayne rolled his window down. "What's going on?"

"The Center is being evacuated. We're advising everyone to go to the new location which is two miles down the road."

"Is the main road closed all the way to Santa Monica?" Dwayne asked.

"I'm not sure sir, but I wouldn't advise driving it. I've heard the flames have reached the edge of the road."

"Okay, thanks man," Dwayne said, falling in line behind the other cars towards the gate.

"Shit, what are we gonna do?" Tammy said, panicking. "We can't get stuck here."

"I agree. We have to pick up Matt and get ready for our next trip." Dwayne pulled out onto the highway and strained to see the road through the thick smoke. The wind howled and sparks from the flying embers continued to dance on the windshield.

Two miles down the highway, they slowed down to a crawl as all the cars in front of them turned into the new evacuation center. Dwayne hesitated before making the turn into the parking lot and looked ahead at the empty highway past where they were supposed to turn into.

Tammy gave him a puzzled look. "What are you doing? This is where we're supposed to go."

"Yeah, but look, the road is clear up ahead. I bet we could make it to Santa Monica and then home."

"But what if the road is closed up ahead?"

The car behind them honked, but Dwayne ignored it." Do you want to give it a go? I don't want to be stranded here. They might make us stay until tomorrow. And what about Matt? If we want to leave for the island in two days, being stuck here will set us back a day."

The car behind them honked perturbedly again. Tammy jerked her head and yelled at the car behind them. "Shut the hell up!" She raised her hands, "I don't know, Dwayne. If you think we can get out of here, then go for it."

He grinned. "Okay, we're outta here."

Tammy grabbed the door handle as Dwayne swerved to get out of the line of traffic and continue down the highway at a steady speed through the thick smoke.

"I hope we've made the right decision. We're the only ones on the road going in this direction." She turned and looked out the window. "I can't even see the ocean and it's right there, this is so eerie."

Dwayne reached over and rubbed her thigh. "We'll be fine. The Santa Monica exit is just a few miles away."

They drove for another mile keeping their eyes peeled, straining to stay focused through the thick smoke.

"The smoke is really thick through here," Tammy said, leaning forward to try and see the road up ahead. She gasped. "Wait! Are those flames I see up ahead?"

Like Tammy, Dwayne leaned forward and looked ahead. "Oh shit! Yes, they're flames alright, right next to the road!" He slowed down the truck as they approached the brush that was on fire next to the road.

"Wait, Dwayne there are flames on both sides of the road!"

Tammy shrieked, pointing to the left where the road had narrowed. "That side is burning too! We can't drive through that!"

Dwayne looked at the burning hillsides. Flames roared high above the truck, on both sides. Flying embers and dark smoke made visibility almost impossible. "I'm going for it! We've made it this far."

"Are you serious? Look at those flames, Dwayne!"

"I can do this; you'll thank me on the other side."

Tammy gave him a snarky grin. "The other side of what? The fire or heaven?"

Dwayne didn't reply and continued to drive towards the burning hillsides. "Brace yourself. As soon as I'm on the edge of the fire I'm going to punch it and race past it."

Tammy picked up Sprity and placed her on her lap; not only did she want to protect her, but she also needed her for comfort. "I don't think I like this. It's not too late to turn around you know," she said, her hands shaking, and her nerves raddled. Tammy gripped the door handle, her heart pounding as they neared the fire. "I can feel the heat from the flames in the truck - this is crazy!"

Dwayne wasn't listening. Without taking his eyes off the road, his hand firmly gripped the steering wheel as he punched the gas pedal and yelled, "hold on!"

Tammy's head hit the back of the seat as he sped off. "Oh, god, this is so damn scary!"

Within seconds they were surrounded by flames on both sides of the truck. Winds blew the flames in all directions, and the crackle of the flames hitting the wind were deafening. Flying embers came from all directions, hitting the windshield, the hood of the truck and the side windows.

"Can you feel that heat?" Tammy screamed. "The windows are so friggin' hot! Give it some more gas and get us the fuck out of here!" she screamed.

Dwayne continued to grip the steering wheel. "My foot is all the way to the floor. I can't see anything ahead of me, just smoke and embers. Man, these flames are huge. Hang on, it has to clear up soon."

Tammy held her breath and leaned back in the seat, her body tense. "I'm afraid these windows may shatter from the heat," she said, her voice shaking as Dwayne continued to race through the burning road.

"Look, the flames are getting smaller." Dwayne pointed to the left, "and on that side, ahead of us, there are no flames." He turned and smiled, "I think we're out of the worst of it."

Tammy released a heavy sigh of relief. "Oh, thank god! I never want to go through anything like that ever again. I've never been so terrified in my entire life, I thought we were goners." She pets the top of Sprity's head. "Even Sprity was nervous, she was digging her claws into my leg."

Dwayne slowed down the truck and glanced at the high flames in his rearview mirror. "Looks like we're in the clear. I see no flames ahead of us, and the smoke is much thinner here. I can see the road ahead of us. We made it! Let's pick up Matt and go home."

Tammy smiled. "That was terrifying. I must say, I have the utmost respect for firefighters now."

TOUR OF A MEGA YACHT

Tour of a Mega Yacht

Some of Tammy's most vivid childhood memories consisted of her dad holding down a full-time job to support his family while chasing his dream of becoming a published author. He would work on his novel into the early hours of the morning in his small office on the top floor of their home. Tammy remembers falling asleep every night to the sound of her father's fingers tapping the keys on his typewriter. He often told her that one day he would quit his job and become a full-time writer. She admired his determination and how he disciplined himself to write every day; even if he was exhausted, he pushed himself to write. Tammy hoped to inherit those qualities from her father when she was older and perhaps even write a book or two someday.

Her father was not a quitter. Tammy admired his determination and the passion that led him to achieve his goals. He stuck to his word and quit his job a few years later and became a successful author. She couldn't be prouder, so when he called her last week and told her that he needed help with some research for his next book, she was flattered.

"What can I possibly help you with, dad?" she asked him.

"Well, the book takes place on a yacht, but not just any yacht - a mega yacht, and I thought you and Dwayne, being knowledgeable when it comes to boats, you'd let me pick your brains a bit. I know absolutely nothing about boats," he laughed. "Any input you can give me would be a tremendous help."

"Of course, Dad. We'd be happy to help. Dwayne knows more than I do, though. He taught me everything I know and he's not here right now. Do you want me to call you when he gets back so you can ask him all the questions you want?"

"Oh, I don't want to do it over the phone. I thought I'd fly out there and stay a couple of days, get a feel for the Marina and the lifestyle, if you know what I mean."

"That would be great, dad! How many years has it been since I've seen you?"

"Too many," John chuckled.

"When were you planning on coming?"

"Next week if that's okay?" her dad replied.

"Fantastic! We'll be ready for you."

Tammy's dad arrived on an evening flight. The next day after a hearty breakfast they headed down to Newport Beach in Tammy's Chevy van.

"Why are we driving to Newport, again?" John asked from the back seat.

"A buddy of mine knows a captain on a mega yacht, and the captain has invited us down for a tour and will gladly answer any questions you may have, John," Dwayne replied with a smile.

"That's fantastic!" John said excitedly, holding up a magazine. He skimmed through the pages with boat listings. "I pictured something like this for the book," he said pointing to a listing of a 125-foot mega yacht, handing it to Tammy.

Tammy held it up to Dwayne. "Isn't that one we're going to see?" she asked.

Dwayne took a quick glance. "Yes, it is! John, that's the boat we're visiting."

John's eyes lit up, "really! Oh, this just keeps getting better and better. I knew I'd asked the right people. I can't believe the one yacht I picked out of this magazine for my book is the one we're going to see. Amazing!"

"Not only that," Dwayne said. "It's docked at the house where John Wayne used to live. It's the only dock big enough for it."

"Wow! We love John Wayne," Tammy shrieked.

"Me too," John echoed. "My favorite movie of course, being Irish, is *The Quiet Man*."

Tammy turned her head and smiled at her dad. "I love that movie too. I didn't know you were a John Wayne fan, dad."

"Oh yes, for many years. Your mom is too."

The drive to Newport took two hours and Dwayne led the way to the dock once they'd arrived. Tammy gasped, walking down the ramp, "is that it?" she said, pointing to the biggest, shiniest white yacht she'd ever seen.

"Yep. Isn't she a beauty?" Dwayne said, leaving the ramp.

"It's bloody massive. No wonder they had to dock it here."

Tammy and her dad followed Dwayne onto the dock where they were met by the captain.

"This is brilliant," John said, looking up at the huge vessel before him. "This is exactly what I pictured for my book."

"Imagine having enough money to buy something like this? One can only dream," Tammy said with dreamy eyes, her neck straining as she looked up at the massive vessel before her.

After shaking hands with the captain, Dwayne introduced him to John. "This is the captain, Tim Snow."

John shook his hand. "It's a pleasure to meet you."

"And this is my girlfriend, Tammy," Dwayne said, smiling at Tammy.

Tammy shook the captain's hand. "Thank you so much for doing this for my dad. She's an amazing yacht."

"Wait till you see the inside," the captain chuckled.

Tammy looked up at the large mansion overlooking the dock. "Was that John Wayne's house?"

"It sure was. He had his boat *The Wild Goose* docked in this very spot. He walked these docks hundreds of times. In fact, he had this dock built specifically to accommodate his boat, and it's the only one in Newport Beach where I can dock this beauty."

"Wow! That gives me goosebumps," Tammy said, rubbing her arms.

"Well, are you ready to come aboard?" the captain asked. "The chef has prepared a wonderful buffet; we can eat lunch, then I'll give you a tour and try to answer any questions you may have, John."

"Oh, I'm sure there'll be many," John said, grinning as he followed everyone up the ramp and onto the yacht.

Tammy held Dwayne's hand as they boarded the luxurious vessel after removing their shoes. They were led to one of the many lavish large teak decks. "God, this place just reeks of money," Tammy whispered, staring at the polished brass bar and the plush blue and white seating against the stern in a half-moon shape.

"There are two more decks: the top one has a large jacuzzi and its own helicopter," the captain told them.

"Is there anything they don't have?" Tammy joked.

"Not really," the captain laughed.

After a lavish buffet consisting of fresh seafood, fruit from all parts of the world and homemade pastries, they spent the next hour touring the yacht.

"I'm afraid to touch anything," Tammy whispered after leaving one of the state rooms. Everything is spotless and shiny and look at all the gold trim."

"Yeah, we'd have to catch a lot of lobsters to afford one of these," Dwayne chuckled.

"I don't think there are enough lobsters in the ocean to buy one of these," Tammy joked. "I mean, look at this place, and this is someone's toy. Imagine what their house looks like; this is luxury at its finest. You can tell no expense was spared. This is amazing!"

They spent a few hours exploring the many luxurious state rooms furnished with the finest bedding and top of the line décor. John was fascinated with the helm and the top-of-the-line navigation system.

"This is stunning," John said, his eyes wide, looking at all the electronics.

Captain Tom began tapping one of the screens. "Here, check this out. What's your address in Ireland?"

John told him his address as Tom typed it into the device. "This is a new system we recently had installed; it's called a GPS chart plotter and it's brilliant," he said, pointing to the screen. "See those numbers?"

John leaned in and looked at the screen. "Yes, what do they mean?"

Tom smiled. "That's the number of miles from this dock to your home in Ireland."

"Really? That's incredible. Technology has sure come a long way in the 90's," he laughed. "I'll definitely be using this in the book. Thank you for showing that to me."

After the tour, including the massive engine room where John drilled the captain with many questions on the mechanics of the yacht (which went right over Tammy's head), they spent the last hour on the lower deck where drinks were served, and Tom answered all of John's questions.

"This was unbelievable. Thank you so much," John said, wearing a huge grin. "I'll be sure to mention you and the yacht in the book and will send you a copy."

"It's been my pleasure. I look forward to reading the book to see if you have been paying attention to what I've shown you," the captain joked.

John held up his notebook and laughed. "I've never filled up a notebook so fast. I can't wait to go through all my notes."

He turned to Dwayne and Tammy, "you've both outdone yourselves on this. You have made this author extremely happy."

Dwayne shook John's hand. "You're welcome. I never realized how much research went into a book. I can't wait to read it either."

"Trust me; if something is not accurate in a book, a reader will point it out and let the author know. I do my best to keep my readers happy."

"Well, it was an honor to be a part of this one, and I look forward to seeing how the book turns out," Dwayne said with a smile.

.

FISHHOOK IN THE MOUTH

$\mathcal{M}$att was ten years old when Dwayne and Tammy took him out on *The Baywitch* for his first Halibut Derby. Just like Dwayne and Tammy, he loved to fish. He brought along Douglas, a buddy from school, who'd never been on a boat before, or even fished. Dwayne was thrilled to be able to give him his first experience.

Also on the boat was their frequent fishing companion, a Jack Russell Terrier named Sprity who was great on the boat, loved the ocean and never failed to show her excitement when it came to fishing. If you lost a fish, she'd jump up on the gunnel and run back and forth barking, expressing her frustrations. When poles were in the water, she would anxiously check each one, standing on her hind legs, looking into the water. If you landed a fish on the boat, Sprity raced around the deck barking with excitement, her tail wagging as she chased the flopping fish across the deck which sometimes was still hooked to the pole.

It was a perfect day for a derby; the ocean was flat with little swell, and the skies a brilliant blue with no clouds. Dwayne picked a spot off Santa Monica to drift for halibut.

Being Douglas' first outing, Dwayne spent extra time coaching him and making sure he was enjoying himself.

Matt landed the first halibut. "I'll be right there with a net!" Dwayne hollered after helping Douglas with his pole. Sprity stood next to Matt on her hind legs, jumping and barking, anxious for the halibut to be brought onto the boat. After grabbing the net, Dwayne raced to Matt's side and scooped the fish into the net. Sprity's excitement level was off the charts as she tried to grab the bottom of the net with her snapping jaw. While fending off the dog, Dwayne managed to remove the hook, retrieve the halibut, and put it in the ice chest. "That's a good size fish, buddy," Dwayne said, giving Matt a high-five. "Do you want more bait?"

"Yes please!" Matt said, his eyes bright.

Dwayne walked over to the bait tank and grabbed a live anchovy, hooking it on Matt's pole. As soon as Sprity saw the small, live fish dangling from the fishing line, she began to jump up and bark incessantly.

"Hold your pole up high," Dwayne instructed Matt as he walked over to the starboard side of the boat. Matt tried his hardest to keep the pole out of Sprity's reach, but his short arms failed him and Sprity managed to grab the small anchovy and take a bite out of it. "Oh no!" Matt squealed. "She got the fish and now she's stuck!" Matt yelled.

"What!" Tammy shrieked, racing over to Sprity.

Dwayne quickly joined her. "Take the pole from Matt," he told Tammy, kneeling to take a closer look.

Tammy took the pole and held it steady. Sprity had stopped jumping and remained perfectly still as Dwayne assessed the situation. The small anchovy had fallen off the hook, but the hook remained in Sprity's mouth and was now stuck. "Shit, it looks like the hook is stuck in her mouth. That's gotta hurt but look how calm she's being. I'm going to cut the line and pick her up so I can take a closer look."

"Okay," Tammy said, watching Dwayne pull out a pocketknife from the back pocket of his jeans and cut the line.

Dwayne gently picked up Sprity, who remained extremely calm, and looked into her mouth. "Yep, it's stuck in there alright. It looks like it went past the barb in her upper lip and into her nasal cavity."

"Oh, shit! Can't you just pull it out?" Tammy asked, cringing at the thought of the hook digging into the flesh of Sprity's mouth.

Dwayne shook his head. "No, not with it going in past the barb. Man, I've never seen this before."

Tammy turned to Matt, "go help Douglas reel in his line and put the pole in the holder. We don't need another fish on the boat right now until we can figure out what to do with Sprity." She then turned to Dwayne. "What are we going to do?" she asked, petting Sprity's back.

"I'm going to get on the marine radio and see if there's anyone, I know out there that may have some tips on getting this hook out. I've never had to deal with this before," he replied, shaking his head.

Tammy took Sprity from Dwayne and placed her on her lap, keeping her hands away from her mouth where the fishing line dangled as Dwayne got on the radio. Within a few minutes a friend of Dwayne's came on the radio. After Dwayne explained the situation to him, he handed the radio over to his friend. "I have no idea what to do, but I have a friend with me who's visiting from Alaska and is an Alaskan fishing guide. I bet he'll know what to do. His name's Mitch."

"Hey Dwayne, Mitch here. So, your dog has a hook stuck in its mouth? Over."

"She sure does. The problem is that it's gone in past the barb. How do I pull it out without ripping half her mouth out? Over."

"Yeah, I've seen this before. What you need to do is use 80-pound test monofilament."

"I have that," Dwayne said eagerly.

"Okay, you need to put it around the shank of the hook and pull it down towards the barb, and at the same time gently pull the hook out."

"Really?" Dwayne said with a creased brow.

"Yeah, it should work," Tom told him. "The heavy monofilament fills up the area behind the barb and displaces the flesh that's behind the barb, then the hook magically pulls out."

"Thanks, man! I'll give it a try and let you know how it goes. I'm out."

After replacing the marina radio microphone in its holder, Dwayne grabbed some 80-pound test line and took a seat on the gunnel of the boat next to Tammy as Matt and Douglas looked on.

"I can't believe how calm she's being. She hasn't moved at all." Tammy said, stroking Sprity's back gently.

"It probably hurts her if she tries to move. Okay, hold her steady while I try to do this," Dwayne told her.

Dwayne followed Tom's instructions precisely and was able to easily pull the hook out. "Wow! It worked, that's amazing!"

As soon as the hook was free from Sprity's mouth, she immediately jumped off Tammy's lap and began barking and running all over the deck. Tammy laughed. "Well, she's happy. Look at her, she's not fazed at all."

Matt and his friend cheered and ran to pet Sprity who continued barking with joy. "Can we fish now?" Matt asked, picking up his pole.

Douglas laughed when Sprity raced over to Matt's pole and began jumping.

"Oh my god! Sprity wants to keep on fishing," Tammy laughed. "The dog has no fear. She's right back at it."

"Well, if she gets hooked again, we now know what to do. Drop your lines boys, we have halibut to catch."

ANOTHER ONE OF TAMMY'S BRILLIANT IDEAS

Fishing for lobsters off the Malibu coastline was not as intense as fishing San Clemente Island. Dwayne and Tammy didn't have to spend seven days away at sea. Malibu was just an hour away, and they were home every night. They could also leave their traps to soak for three days, as there was no threat of sheepshead swimming into the traps and eating the lobsters as there was at the island. It was one of the reasons why the traps had to be pulled every day at the island. If they got an early start, another bonus, fishing Malibu was that they'd be back at the dock in time to pick Matt up from school.

On one particular trip, they had left early in the *Little Boat* and were off to a good start. The ocean was calm with small swells and just a bit of wind. A few clouds scattered the skies, and the lobsters were plentiful. Dwayne and Tammy were having a good day and were in a great mood.

"I wish all days were like this," Tammy hollered from where she stood next to a trap they'd just pulled, measuring lobsters.

Dwayne looked over his shoulder from his seat at the helm. "Yeah, me too. But I do see some clouds beginning to roll in and the wind is starting to pick up. Hopefully, we'll have all our traps pulled before it gets any worse."

Tammy placed a legal lobster in the barrel of saltwater on the boat, tossing two shorts over the side back into the ocean. "Oh, don't say that. We still have two-thirds of our traps to pull."

"We'll speed up our pace a bit and try to stay ahead of the weather. There weren't any weather warnings this morning, but we both know how quickly that can change," he chuckled.

Tammy rolled her eyes. "Oh, don't remind me."

They were travelling north to their next trap, and by the time they'd reached it, the skies had turned a dark grey, the winds had increased, and the swells had doubled in size.

"Well, this sucks!" Tammy yelled above the loud sound of the outboard motor, trying to avoid getting splashed in the face by ocean spray. "You jinxed it," she hollered to Dwayne, who was now standing up to gain better control of the boat.

"Let's pull the next trap and figure out what we're going to do next. The winds must be blowing at least 30 miles an hour."

Tammy grabbed the gaff from its holder as Dwayne slowed the boat down near the buoy of their next trap. Her body rocked from the continuing bashing of waves as she grabbed the teak handle on the trap table to steady herself. "God it's getting rough out here."

"Don't miss the trap!" Dwayne hollered. "It'll be a bitch to come around on it again in these winds."

"I'll do my best!" Tammy hollered, getting into position with her one arm stretched out holding the gaff and the other holding tightly onto the teak handle of the trap table. The *Little Boat* rocked hard, slamming against the waves. Tammy leaned forward at the waist and quickly turned her head to avoid the huge wave of water that drenched her. "Damn it!"

"Okay, grab it now!" Dwayne yelled.

Tammy leaned further, then with one swift move that she'd done hundreds of times before, hooked the line with the gaff, pulled it in and quickly fed the line through the puller. "Got it!" she shouted. "Damn that was hard, and I'm soaked," she yelled, wiping her face with her sleeve.

"I'm not sure if we should pull any more traps. The Santa Ana winds are blowing offshore, and they're really picking up."

Tammy put the last lobster from the trap in the barrel with a furrowed brow. "Well, what are we supposed to do? We can't bob around out here, and we haven't pulled many traps."

"We're almost at Little Dume and Point Dume. There's a small cove between the two where I can drop anchor. There we'll be sheltered and protected from these winds. We can hang out there for a while until the weather dies down."

Tammy nodded. "Sounds like a good idea to me. It's freezing out here with these winds blowing."

After dropping the trap back into the water, Tammy joined Dwayne at the helm where she was shielded from the constant spray of water and increasing winds.

"How far away are we?" she asked.

"We'll be there in about ten minutes; it'll be a lot calmer there."

"Good, my hands are killing me from holding on, not to mention my knees."

Dwayne gave her a caring smile. "We're almost there, then you'll be able to relax for a bit."

When Dwayne entered the small cove, the waters instantly became calmer, and the winds settled into a slight breeze. Ocean spray no longer crested over the bow, and Tammy released her hold on the rail of the dash.

"Oh, this is much better," Tammy smiled, feeling relieved. "This was a good idea."

When they were 50 feet from shore, Tammy helped Dwayne set the anchor. Once he'd turned off the motor, Tammy welcomed the silence. "It's pretty here. We never get to see the shoreline up close cause we're always so busy pulling traps," she said, grabbing two sodas from the ice chest and handing one to Dwayne.

"Yeah, it sure is peaceful compared to out there. Look at all those whitecaps. I'm glad we came; we're protected in here."

"How long do you want to stay here?" Tammy asked, looking around.

Dwayne shrugged his shoulders. "I don't know. Maybe an hour?"

Tammy scanned the deck, "what do you want to do for an hour?"

Dwayne laughed. "We're doing it. You always have to be doing something," he said, leaning back in the captain's chair. "You need to learn how to relax."

"I am relaxed." She looked at the sandy cove onshore. "How about we relax over there? We can lay out on the sand and get warm. It's nice and calm in here."

"And how are we supposed to get there?"

"We'll swim, of course. It's not that far."

Dwayne gave Tammy a hard stare. "Are you serious? You want to swim over there?"

Tammy walked over to where Dwayne sat and stood before him, wrapping her arms around his neck. "Yes, it'll be fun. We can strip down, put our clothes, towels and some snacks in a black trash bag so they'll stay dry, then swim to shore. What do you say? Tell me you wouldn't want to laze in the sun rather than sit on this boat and do nothing?"

Dwayne shook his head. "You're impossible. I can't believe you're seriously considering this."

"I'm not considering it; I want to do it." She gave him a nudge on the arm. "Come on, please? It'll be a blast."

Dwayne raised his hands in defeat. "Okay. If you really want to do this, why don't you go find us two trash bags; we'll take one each so they're not too heavy and I'll start stripping down."

"Yes!" Tammy squealed. "I'll be right back."

When Tammy returned with two bags and two towels, Dwayne was already naked, his clothes rolled up and ready to put in a trash bag.

"Well, hey sexy," Tammy said, approaching Dwayne and kissing him tenderly on the lips. "We should try fishing naked."

"Hell no!" Dwayne laughed. "Wire traps, gaffs, hooks and a slippery deck, I don't think so! Come on, get undressed and put your clothes in a bag. I'm getting chilly standing here."

Within minutes Tammy had her clothes and towel in a plastic bag. She opened the ice chest to grab some snacks. "How about orange juice, granola bars and chips?" she asked.

"Sounds good to me," Dwayne replied.

Tammy tied her bag and stepped up on the gunnel of the *Little Boat* and looked at the water. "Are you ready?" she said, looking at Dwayne standing next to her holding his bag.

"As ready as I'll ever be."

"Let's jump in together on the count of three."

Dwayne nodded. "Okay."

Tammy turned and faced the water, bending at the knees. "One, two and three."

Together they dove into the water and immediately released a loud, piecing scream. "Oh my god, the water is so frigging cold!" Tammy screamed, racing to shore.

"It's so cold, it hurts," Dwayne yelled, swimming as fast as he could behind her.

"My god! It stings. My fingers are numb," Tammy yelled, swimming as fast as she could.

When she was able to touch the bottom, relief set in knowing she would be out of the frigid water soon. She ran through the water holding the black bag tightly above her head to ensure everything stayed dry.

Dwayne was close behind. When they reached the shore, Tammy dropped her bag and untied it as fast as she could, her hands aching from the cold. Her body shivered from head to toe as she yanked out the towel. "Thank god it's dry," she squealed, wrapping it around her body. "I'm so bloody cold."

Shivering, Dwayne mirrored her actions and quickly wrapped

himself in his towel. "How did you ever talk me into this? I'm so friggin' cold."

"I didn't know the water would be so damn cold," Tammy barked.

"It must be about 55 degrees, that's too damn cold to be swimming in." Dwayne held out his arms, "come here, I'll warm you up."

Still bundled in her towel, Tammy leaned into Dwayne's embrace and rested her head on his chest. She shivered when she spoke. "I'm freezing."

Keeping his towel around his shoulders, Dwayne wrapped the two of them up and rubbed her shoulders vigorously. "Give it a minute and you'll start to warm up."

"I can't feel my feet," Tammy moaned, keeping her head buried against Dwayne's chest.

"That was a crazy idea you had. Are you getting any warmer?"

Tammy nodded. "Yeah," pulling away from his embrace and looking up to the skies. "Well at least there are no clouds here. We can lay out and get warm." Tammy unraveled her body from the towel and laid on the sand. After laying down, she patted the ground next to her. "Come join me. The heat from the sun feels good, I'm beginning to warm up."

Dwayne placed his towel next to hers and felt the warmth from the rays of the sun on his skin as soon as he laid down. "Oh, much better," he said, his eyes closed.

"See, this is what I had in mind. Doesn't this feel good?" Tammy said. "Much better than sitting on the *Little Boat* bored out of our minds."

Dwayne chuckled. "I'm not going to argue with that." He sat up and checked on the boat. It was anchored in a protective area of the cove, but beyond it he could clearly see that the ocean was covered with whitecaps, stirred up by the Santa Ana winds blowing offshore. "It does look pretty nasty out there."

After an hour of relaxing on the sandy beach, their bodies toasty warm, Dwayne sat up. "It's still pretty nasty out there, but we should get back to the boat and see if we can pull more traps."

"Oh, but this feels so good," Tammy moaned, still lying on her back.

"I know, I'd love to stay here too, but we really need to get back on the boat."

Tammy moaned again, "fine," and sat up. "Wow, it's so calm in this cove compared to out there."

"That's because it's protected by the two hillsides on either side," he said, standing up and shaking his towel.

Tammy also stood up and shook her towel before putting it in the plastic bag.

"Are you ready?" Dwayne asked, holding his bag over his shoulder.

Tammy walked to where the ocean met the sand and stared at the frigid cold waves breaking on shore. "Oh crap, I don't want to get back in the water. It's freezing."

"We don't have a choice," Dwayne laughed. Tammy walked out up to her knees and quickly ran out. "It's too damn cold! At least when we jumped off the boat, we cleared at least ten feet of water. This is much harder, walking out like this."

Dwayne laughed again and proceeded to walk out, but as soon as a wave splashed him above his waist, he raced back to shore. "Man! It's so cold it stings," he yelled.

"See, I told you. It's too damn cold and look how far we have to swim."

"I hear you. I'm already freezing and I'm not even in the water," Dwayne complained.

Tammy tried again and tiptoed out into the water, but as soon as it reached her thigh she quickly turned around and raced back to shore. "I can't do this! What the hell are we going to do?"

Dwayne laughed. "This is another brilliant idea of yours that has gotten us into a pickle. I need to stop listening to you," he joked.

"Hey, not all my ideas are bad, but this one is up there. Shit Dwayne, there's no way I can swim back to the boat. It's much farther than when we jumped off." Dwayne looked up at the hillside behind them and heard cars going by on Pacific Coast Highway. "The only other option I can think of would be that I climb that hill, hitch a ride back to the marina, and bring *The Baywitch* here. I can tie up next to the *Little Boat,* bring it in closer to shore to pick you up, then tow the *Little Boat* behind the *Baywitch* back to the marina."

"Oh, that could take hours!" Tammy screamed.

"Do you have any other ideas?"

Tammy looked out at the ocean again and watched the whitecaps beyond the *Little Boat.* "Man, I guess we're going to have to grin and bear the cold and just go for it."

"Okay, then. Well, the sooner we get in the water, the sooner it'll be over."

Tammy took a deep breath and inched her toes into the water. "Okay, let's do this!"

"Okay, I'm right behind you. Swim as fast as you can to the stern of the boat and pull yourself up with the rope hanging over the side."

Tammy nodded, her knees now submerged in the water, her body tense from the freezing temperatures. Holding out her arms, she held the bag high in one hand as she held her breath from the frigid water freezing her thighs. "It's so friggin' cold!" she screamed. "Screw this! It's torture. I'm going for it!" Without hesitating, Tammy dove into the water, submerging her entire body up to her neck. "Fuck! It's freezing!" she screamed at the top of her lungs, frantically kicking her feet and swimming as fast as she could with one free hand while the other held the plastic bag above her head.

While swimming hard towards the *Little Boat,* Tammy continued to scream, her body rigid from the cold. Close behind her was Dwayne, also expressing his pain from the frigid water.

When Tammy reached the stern, she quickly grabbed the line with one hand dangling in the water, and with the other hand managed to toss the bag over the stern and into the boat. Using all her strength, she immediately pulled herself onto the boat with the aid of the line. Shivering, she clasped her hands in front of her chest and bent her knees to brace herself from the continuous rocking of the boat, waiting for Dwayne to get to the stern. "Come on, you're almost there!" she yelled.

Dwayne reached the boat within seconds, tossing his bag over the edge and onto the boat, which Tammy grabbed and threw out of the way. Dwayne pulled himself out of the water. "Fuck! Never again. I almost had a heart attack, I swear."

Once Tammy saw that Dwayne was safely on the boat, she raced into the small cabin and grabbed two blankets which were piled in the front. When she returned to the deck, Dwayne was in the process of ripping open his bag, shivering.

"Screw the towels," Tammy yelled, handing him a blanket, and wrapping herself another. "These will warm us up quicker."

"Thanks," Dwayne said, his lips quivering.

Embraced by the warmth of the blanket, Tammy paced the deck to warm up her feet that were still stinging. "Man, I've never felt so damn cold in my life, that was horrible!"

Dwayne steadied himself at the helm, still wrapped in the blanket. The Santa Anas continued to attack the ocean as the white caps continued to blanket the outer waters.

"Yeah, never again. Next time we find ourselves in harsh weather, we stay on the boat or head back in. Captain's orders," he laughed.

Tammy gave him a salute. "You've got no arguments from me."

"Speaking of fishing, we're done for the day. Enough of this shit."

Tammy smiled. "Spoken like a true Captain. Let's get dressed and pull up anchor."

BOAT CRASH

When Dwayne and Tammy bought their new boat, *The Baywitch II*, it was a game changer for them. An efficient boat with a single diesel engine instead of twin gas engines would drastically cut their fuel costs alone. The spacious deck transported traps much cheaper, and the hull's smooth lines made the crossing smoother.

What the boat did lack was cosmetics; she was in dire need of a new paint job that would make her shine and reveal her true beauty. The deck also needed some attention, and they had plans to take some time off fishing in the near future and bring the boat up to ship shape condition.

When they moved out of the boatyard and rented a house nearby, they kept the *Little Boat* on a trailer at the house until it was sold a few months later and rented space at the fuel dock for *The Baywitch II.*

Life was good, fishing was profitable, expenses were down, and life had become less stressful. When it came time to giving The *Baywitch II* a makeover, Dwayne and Tammy worked around the clock prepping, sanding, priming, and painting the boat, as well as refinishing the deck and making fiberglass repairs as needed. The tasks were not cheap, but the rewards were priceless.

"She looks like a brand new boat," Tammy said, standing on the dock with Dwayne and admiring the hull with its new, shiny grey paint job.

"She sure does. Much better than the faded ugly blue color she had when we bought her."

Along with Dwayne and Tammy, the boat was well known in the Marina. When she was back at the fuel dock in her regular spot after her makeover, she didn't go unnoticed. *The Baywitch II* was striking, and an eye catcher as well, once it was in its regular spot at the end of the fuel dock. Fellow boaters couldn't resist taking a walk down the docks to take a closer look at the beautiful vessel and chat with Dwayne about the work he'd done, if he happened to be there.

When it came to boats, there was nothing Dwayne didn't know. It was something Tammy admired about him. He bought a diamond in the rough, saw the enormous potential the boat had, and made it shine. Tammy couldn't believe the transformation, and neither could those that had seen the boat before and after. Some even questioned if it was the same boat!

Later in the season, they now were fishing for lobsters off Malibu and didn't need to go out every day. And with the makeover of *The Baywitch II* complete, they were able to spend more time at home working on gear in the backyard. Tammy was clipping doors to traps while Dwayne loaded finished traps into his truck to take down to *The Baywitch II* and take them out to Malibu on his next trip. Just then the phone on the patio table rang.

"I'll get it," Dwayne said, taking off his gloves. "Dwayne here," he said, picking up the phone.

Tammy stopped using the air tool so that Dwayne could hear his call and was shocked when he started cursing into the phone.

"What do you mean she got hit? How much damage is there and who hit her?" Dwayne continued, cussing as the other person spoke. "Damn it! This is fucking bullshit. I'll be right down!" he yelled, hanging up and slamming the phone down onto the table.

Tammy raced over to his side. "What the hell is going on? Who got hit?"

"Our boat! One of those giant sportfishing boats hit *The Baywitch II*! Shit! We gotta go to the fuel dock. Grab your stuff and let's go."

Tammy gasped. "Oh no! After all our hard work. Come on, let's just go. I don't need anything."

After speeding through town and running a few red lights, they made it to the fuel dock in about five minutes. A crowd was gathered around *The Baywitch II,* and Dwayne jumped out of the truck. Fueled with anger, blood boiling, he raced down the ramp to the dock and pushed through the crowd of people.

Unable to keep up with him, Tammy reached the dock a few minutes later, and, like Dwayne, pushed herself through the people until she was next to him. From the dock the damage couldn't be seen. They'd been told that the port side of the boat had been hit which faced out onto the water.

Dwayne stepped onto the boat and marched over to the port side and leaned over to take a look. "Holy shit! They took out the whole damn side. It's completely destroyed."

Tammy followed close behind and leaned over the side and gasped. "Oh my god! It's ruined."

Dwayne raked his hands through his hair and clenched his fist. "Thank god it was hit above the waterline, otherwise this boat would be sinking right about now."

Tammy had never seen him so angry and wasn't sure what to do.

"God damn motherfuckers!" Dwayne yelled at the top of his lungs. "They just put me out of fucking business."

"I cannot believe this just happened! We *just* got done painting it and redoing the deck," Tammy cried.

Dave, the owner of the fuel dock, stepped onto the boat. Dwayne quickly spun around, his nostrils flared. "What the hell happened, Dave?"

Dave pointed out to the main channel where a large sportfishing boat was being towed. "That 50-foot sportfishing boat hit you."

"How?" Dwayne snapped.

"From what I understand, it was in reverse and the cable broke. They couldn't get it out of reverse, and it rammed right into your boat. I'm sorry, man. It happened so fast."

"So, what the hell am I supposed to do now? The whole port side is caved in. I can't fish, there's too much damage. How the hell am I supposed to make any money?"

Dave rested his hand on Dwayne's shoulder, trying to calm him down. "I'm sure they have insurance and will pay for all of the repairs."

Dwayne waved his hands in the air, shaking Dave's hand off his shoulder. "Have you ever tried to deal with insurance companies? That could take months. I don't have months to sit around waiting for them to get around to my case. By law, I have to pull my traps every 96 hours. If I don't, I could be fined and lose my permit, then I'll be out of a job. This is fucking bullshit!" he barked, pacing the dock. "I'm going over there right now to give him a piece of my mind."

Dave raised his hand, "Dwayne, I don't think that's a good idea. The way you're feeling right now, you'll probably punch the guy, and we don't want that to happen. You need to calm down and get on the phone with your insurance company."

"Dave's right," Tammy said, standing behind them. "Let's go home and make some phone calls, then when you've calmed down, we'll come back and talk to the captain of the sportfishing boat."

For the first time since arriving at the dock, Dwayne cracked a joke. "Can't I have just one punch?"

Tammy giggled, relieved he was starting to calm down. "No. After you've checked out the damage on our boat, we'll go home so you can report it to the insurance company."

They spent the next hour assessing the brutal damage, their hearts crushed, and concerns about how they were going to make a living weighed heavily on their minds.

"We are so fucked!" Dwayne said, sitting outside at home after talking to the insurance company. "I told them that this is our livelihood, and as long as the boat is out of commission, we're out of a job. They didn't seem to care. I even told them that I have to pull my traps every 96 hours, and she said they'd file a claim. Just the stupid routine that they do for everyone." He leaned back in his chair and tossed back his head, running his hands through his hair. "God, I hate insurance companies."

For the next few days, Dwayne and Tammy were at a loss as to what to do next. The insurance company of the sportfishing boat was giving them the runaround, and Dwayne was stressed about not being able to pull their traps. "If we don't get out there soon, Fish & Game is going to be on our ass. What are we supposed to do if we lose our permit?"

"I wish we still had the *Little Boat*," Tammy said. "We could have used that."

"Yeah, but we don't, and we have to think of something soon. I'm not going to play this waiting game with the stupid insurance companies. Our livelihood is at stake." He slammed his hand down on the patio table, startling Tammy. "You know what? I have a big shot attorney friend. He's well known in the Marina. I'm going to give him a call, maybe he can help."

"Dwayne, we can't afford an attorney."

"The guy owes me a favor," he chuckled. "I've worked on his yacht and done many favors for him. He's even said that if I ever need his help to give him a call."

Tammy grinned; hope seeping from her eyes. "Then what are you waiting for? Give him a call. What do we have to lose? We're desperate here."

"I'll be right back. I'm going to call him right now."

In less than ten minutes, Dwayne returned, smiling.

"Well, you look better than when you left. Good news I hope?"

"I told him everything, including that our livelihood is at risk. He said to let him handle it and he'll get back to me in a day or so."

Tammy's eyes grew wide. "Wow, really! I wonder what he'll do?"

Dwayne folded his arms. "I have no idea, but I do know he's a damn good attorney and knows his stuff. I have faith in the man. You should have heard the excitement in his voice after I told him everything. He sounded pretty confident that he could help us."

"But what can he do in a day? Our boat can't be fixed that quickly, and we need to go fishing."

"We'll just have to wait and see, but he told me not to worry, and that it'll all work out. I have to believe the man, otherwise I'll go crazy."

The next day Jerry, the attorney, kept his promise and called Dwayne, asking him to meet him at his office in an hour.

"Shit! Let me go change, I want to go with you," Tammy said excitedly, throwing down the brush she was using to paint buoys.

"Okay, but don't take too long, I don't want to miss him."

"Just give me five minutes," she hollered, racing to the bedroom.

It was only a five-minute ride to Jerry's office, and he greeted them with a friendly smile and a firm handshake. "Have a seat, guys."

Dwayne sat with his back straight and his hands gripping the wooden handles of the chair. "So, what did you find out?" he asked.

Jerry smiled again and opened a file in front of him. "Well Dwayne, you've known me for a long time, and you know that I don't mess around or take any bullshit from anyone." He handed

Dwayne a check. "This is for you. It's a check for $15,000 to pay for the damage to your boat."

Dwayne's jaw dropped and Tammy gasped. "Oh, wow! I don't know what to say," Dwayne said, stunned. "How did you get them to pay up so fast?"

Jerry leaned back in his chair. "Like I said, I don't take any bullshit, and believe me, they tried to give me the runaround, but I wasn't having it. As soon as I mentioned that your livelihood was threatened and they could either pay for the repairs to your boat *or* pay for the loss of your livelihood for the rest of your life, they changed their tune." He smiled again. "And that's not all…"

"It isn't?" Dwayne said, his voice flat, still shocked by the check he was holding in his hand.

"Nope. I also informed them about the legalities of your career and what laws you must abide by, and that you're in jeopardy of losing your permit because you have no boat to pull your gear due to them hitting it, and I offered them a solution."

Dwayne looked at Jerry with his brow furrowed. "You did? What's that?"

"If you know of a fellow fisherman that will take you out to pull your traps, the insurance company of the sportfishing boat has agreed to pay the owner of the boat each time he takes you out until your boat's fixed."

"Wow, I don't know what to say. You sure don't mess around."

"Do you know of someone that can take you out to pull your gear?" Jerry asked.

"Yeah, I know plenty of guys that would be willing to help. This is amazing, you really saved the day!"

"Yes, thank you so much!" Tammy added.

"No problem, guys. I always keep my word, Dwayne. There's been many times when you've come to my rescue, fixing my yacht on a last minute's notice." He hesitated and grinned. "But there is one thing you can do for me."

"Sure, anything. What is it?" Dwayne said.

"Bring me a couple of lobsters once you've got your boat running again."

Dwayne smiled and shook his hand. "It would be my pleasure. Anytime you want lobsters, they're on me."

LOST IN THE FOG

After a few years of fishing for lobsters, Dwayne and Tammy became a good team and worked well together. They knew their places on the boat, the tasks involved, and had reached a point where they felt confident that they could try and increase their catch. They were pulling traps faster, and decided they would double up on traps, spending hours working through the night building more of them, which also meant painting more buoys, building more bait compartments, and buying more bait.

Because of the extra load and the time needed to pull all the gear, they decided for the first trip to Malibu they would take both *The Baywitch* and the *Little Boat.* They would use *The Baywitch* to carry the extra gear and spend the night in Paradise Cove off Malibu so they could spend two days pulling traps. They would use the *Little Boat* to pull the gear because it could fish in shallow waters.

Once *The Baywitch* was safely anchored in Paradise Cove, they got an early start. Dwayne and Tammy wasted no time loading up the *Little Boat* with snacks and traps from *The Baywitch* to start a full day of fishing, pulling as many traps as they could before the sun went down. The rest they'd pull tomorrow.

"Let's go Tammy, the clock's ticking," Dwayne hollered from the helm of the *Little Boat* which was side tied to *The Baywitch*.

"I'm coming!" Tammy yelled over the roar of the *Little Boat's* motor. "Let me get my slickers on." After tightening her shoulder straps, she jumped onto the *Little Boat* and untied the lines securing it to *The Baywitch* and pushed them off.

Dwayne put the boat in gear and sped off towards the first trap.

"It's a gorgeous day out here," Tammy said, standing behind Dwayne, a slight breeze blowing through her hair, tickling the back of her neck. It was a weekday, and the ocean was quiet with very few boats. She never got tired of looking at the greatness of the ocean and the freedom it provided, especially on days like this when the swells were small and the winds light.

"It sure is," Dwayne replied, looking for their first buoy. "But I do see a fog bank rolling in."

Tammy looked ahead. "Oh wow! Where did that come from? It doesn't look very far away."

"Hopefully, it won't be too thick. I see the first trap coming up. Let's hustle and get as many traps pulled as we can and hope the fog lifts."

For the next hour, Dwayne and Tammy worked diligently until it became impossible to see the next buoy up ahead. "I can't see a damn thing," Dwayne complained, leaning forward over the dash while steering the *Little Boat.*

"Me neither," Tammy said, looking out over the starboard side. "We're surrounded by fog."

Dwayne slowed down the boat so he could get his bearings. "Well, I guess that fog bank reached us, and it isn't light. If anything, I think it's gotten thicker. I can't see 20 feet in front of the boat. This is really eerie."

"I'll say," Tammy replied. "I don't think I like this. I feel like a sea monster is going to jump out of the ocean or something," she joked.

Dwayne laughed. "You have such an imagination. You should write a book."

"And when would I have time to do that?" said Tammy sarcastically.

Dwayne put the boat in neutral and glanced at their surroundings. "I can't see the coastline either. There's no way we're going to be able to pull any more traps. We have zero visibility, it's too dangerous."

"So, what should we do?" Tammy asked, her hands on her hips.

"I guess head back to *The Baywitch* and wait it out."

Tammy stomped her feet. "Seriously? But that'll set us back. How long will it take for this damn fog to lift?"

Dwayne put the boat in gear, turned around and started heading back in the direction from where they came. After a few minutes he slowed the boat down and furrowed his brow.

"What's the matter?" Tammy asked, joining him at the helm.

"I have no idea where *The Baywitch* is, my sense of direction is distorted from all this fog."

"Oh, shit! Well, we didn't go that far down the line. We can't be too far away from it."

"Yes, but in what direction? I can't tell which is north or south. I don't have a radar on this boat, and I didn't take the GPS coordinates of *The Baywitch,* I didn't think I'd need them. We're anchored at Paradise Cove, a place I've used for years. But out here in this dense fog, it could be in any direction."

Tammy strained her eyes, trying to make sense of everything around them, hoping to see some sort of shoreline, but it was hopeless. "I can't see anything."

"Me neither," Dwayne said. *The Baywitch* could be 50 feet away from us and we wouldn't even know it."

"What the hell are we going to do? This fog could stick around for the rest of the day. I don't want to be bobbing around out here in it. We may hit something; or worse, something may hit us."

"I'm going to keep driving around. Keep your eyes peeled for anything that looks like a boat."

As Dwayne crawled along at a low speed through the fog, Tammy stood on the port side without taking her eyes off the desolate ocean and the thick bank of fog that engulfed them.

"See anything?" Dwayne hollered after 30 minutes had passed.

Tammy shook her head. "Nope, not a damn thing. I have no idea where we are. This is like looking for a needle in a haystack. I have no idea what direction *The Baywitch* may be in, and I'm starting to get worried, Dwayne." Tammy scanned their surroundings again. "We might be heading out to sea, away from the coastline for all we know."

"I'm going to keep driving around for a while. We don't have a choice."

"Okay," Tammy moaned, continuing to stare out at the ocean.

Another 30 minutes passed, and Dwayne released a heavy sigh as he put the boat in neutral. "This is ridiculous."

"Well, what else can we do?"

"I have an idea."

"What's that?" Tammy asked, anxious to hear.

"Well, I know that we anchored *The Baywitch* in 40 feet of water."

Her brow furrowed, Tammy cried, "what good does that do us? We're not on *The Baywitch*."

"No, we're not, but I have a fish finder on this boat that will show me the depth of the water we're in. If I get us to 40 feet of water and stay at that depth in either direction, we should reach *The Baywitch* at some point."

Tammy smiled. "You're brilliant! It makes perfect sense to me now."

Anxiously, Dwayne turned on the fish finder, then once they were in 40 feet of water, he steered the boat in a straight line.

"Now, keep your eyes peeled. I don't want to hit *The Baywitch*. It should suddenly appear in this thick fog."

Tammy leaned out, keeping her eyes peeled and looking in all directions. "Come on *Baywitch,* where are you?" she whispered under her breath, hoping it would pop out of the fog.

"Anything yet?" Dwayne hollered, steering the boat cautiously.

"Nothing yet." Then Tammy screamed, jumping up and down and pointing her finger. "I see it! I see it! Over there."

Dwayne focused on where she was pointing and grinned as soon as he saw the outline of *The Baywitch*. "I see it too, thank god! I was beginning to have doubts that we'd ever find her."

Tammy grabbed the line, ready to tie off the *Little Boat* to *The Baywitch,* smiling at Dwayne. "That was a fantastic idea you had."

Dwayne grinned. "Yeah, I just wished I'd thought of it sooner. We spent over an hour looking, but hey, if we ever find ourselves in this predicament again, which I hope we never do, I know what to do!"

DON'T LET GO!

One of the fisheries Tammy never got involved in was spot prawns, and she'd always worry when Dwayne went out on his own. It wasn't a fishery he did often, but when he did, it was in deep waters far off the coastline.

Many times, he'd return to the dock, as Tammy anxiously awaited his safe return, with an adventurous tale to tell.

Tammy knew that commercial fishing was one of the most dangerous industries, and when you're out on the vast, unforgiving ocean by yourself, it becomes twice as dangerous.

When Dwayne returned after one such trip, Tammy became horrified as Dwayne told her the hair-raising events of the day while sitting on the deck, his voice still shaking as he spoke.

It began when Tammy noticed he was wearing one boot. After grabbing him a Pepsi from the ice chest, she looked down and said, "Hey, where's your other boot?"

Dwayne released a nervous chuckle. "At the bottom of the ocean."

Tammy's jaw dropped. "What? How did that happen?" she asked, taking a seat next to him.

Dwayne leaned back in his seat. "Man, it happened so fast I thought I was a goner. I was fishing out deep like I always do in a canyon, 1,200 to 1,500 feet deep. As you know, I took 30 traps, and I used 6,000 feet of line laying on the deck. Two thousand feet of upline that goes from the buoy to the first anchor, and 2,000 feet of line that lays across the bottom of the ocean that I clip the traps to and goes to the second anchor, then another 2,000 feet of upline to the surface and a second set of buoys. I was setting the line and had 15 traps in the water and 15 more to go. I had the boat on autopilot while I was clipping the traps to the line, and the coil of line on the deck was feeding into the ocean with a clipped trap." Dwayne took a deep breath. "Everything was going great. I had a rhythm going, because by doing everything yourself and making sure everything runs smoothly, there's no time to stop. But as I was clipping the traps and walking back and forth over a deck covered with line, my boot got tangled up with the line that was being pulled into the ocean."

"Oh my god!" Tammy shrieked. "How did you get your boot off?"

"Well, that was the scary part. I couldn't. The rope was getting tighter and tighter. I managed to reach over to the helm, and when I tried to put the boat in neutral, my leg got pulled up into the air. As I tried to save myself, my hand fell on the throttle. Now the boat was going faster, and I was being pulled to the stern."

Tammy's jaw dropped. "Shit! What'd you do?"

"I honestly thought that this was it - this is how I'm going to die. I'm going to be pulled overboard and die at the bottom of the ocean and no one will ever find me. My heart was racing like crazy, and the rope was like a choker around my boot. I held onto any part of the boat I could as the rope kept pulling me closer to what I now saw as certain death. There was no way I could reach the throttle to slow the boat down, and no way I could loosen the line around my boot, but I wasn't about to give up without a fight. I hollered and screamed, determined not to let the line beat me. I was forcedly being pulled to the back of the boat until my leg was hanging over the stern. Every second I could feel the line getting tighter - it felt like death was knocking at my door. My voice was hoarse from yelling, and my hands were beginning to cramp up from holding on to anything I could, but there was no way I was gonna let go. Then suddenly my boot just popped off my foot from the force of the line and I watched as it splashed into the ocean. I immediately raced to the helm and put the boat in neutral."

"Oh my god, Dwayne. This is what I'm always afraid of when you go out alone. Especially in those deep waters - you could have drowned."

Dwayne took another deep breath. "I know, that was a narrow escape. I just sat there on the boat, trying to catch my breath. My chest was heaving, and my hands were shaking. I honestly couldn't move. I think I was in shock for a while. It took me a while to function again and bring my heart rate back to normal." He finally cracked a smile. "I've never felt so happy to be back here sitting on this boat with you as I do now."

Tammy smiled and leaned in, resting her head on his chest. "Me neither. I don't want to hear any more horror stories like that again."

Dwayne laughed. "Oh, it's just another day's work, fishing on the ocean," he joked.

DON'T BELIEVE EVERYTHING YOU SEE

When making a nine-hour night crossing from San Clemente Island to the mainland, Dwayne and Tammy would always drive in two-hour shifts, allowing them to each get some much-needed rest on the trip home and be alert at the helm when it was their turn.

Tammy hated traveling at night but understood that it was necessary. With a boat full of live lobsters, no time could be wasted waiting for daylight to head back home. Every minute was crucial, and valuable time was spent checking the catch and ensuring they made the long journey home alive before being sold within hours after tying up at the dock.

Traveling at night was a time when Tammy felt the vastness of the ocean and at its most vulnerable. It was dark, eerie, and desolate, and boy did she feel small. When it was her shift, she never left the helm, not even for a bottle of water from the ice chest. If she forgot to grab one before tending the helm, she'd wait until her shift was over. She was afraid that if she left for just a few seconds, they'd hit a floating log or other debris, things you wouldn't see until it was too late. Tammy held the wheel tight, keeping her eyes peeled on the ocean before her, constantly looking in all directions for any kind of floating items that may cross their path. She had to always be on alert and taking short shifts like Dwayne had suggested ensured that.

Whenever Dwayne ended his time at the wheel, he made sure Tammy knew their course and read it correctly on the compass, along with going over what to look for on the radar. "If you see any blinking green dots, it means there's probably a boat up ahead, and you need to slow down and keep a look out." He would always give her a hard stare. "Understood?"

"Yeah, I got it, and I'll wake you if I see anything."

Left alone at the wheel Tammy remained focused, checking the radar and compass constantly. She had mastered the art of staying on course, thanks to a tip Dwayne had given her when she first started fishing.

"Pick a star and follow it. They never move and they'll take you home," he told her.

Tammy tried it, and miraculously it worked. She then began calling them her guiding stars. After checking the equipment on the dash, Tammy picked her star and made herself comfortable at the helm.

She was driving the last leg of their journey, and everything was going well. No mishaps or strange floating objects in the ocean. She'd been keeping watch for just over an hour, and they were about three miles out from the main harbor entrance of the Marina. In about half an hour they'd be tying up to the dock and she could relax.

Tammy checked the radar again and noticed a dot on the screen that wasn't there a few minutes ago. "What the hell?" she whispered under her breath. She leaned forward at the dash and searched for any lights that might be a boat up ahead. She saw nothing - no red port light or green starboard light. Tammy looked at the radar again and gasped. The green light was gone. She creased her brow. "What the hell?" She leaned out of the side of the boat and looked sharply all around her. "This makes no sense. It's not on the radar." She looked behind her and saw only a dark, empty ocean. "Where the hell did it go?"

Feeling nervous, Tammy grabbed the wheel with both hands and checked the radar again. She was horrified to see another dot blinking on the screen and then, just as quickly, disappear. "What the hell is going on? How many boats are out here, and why do they keep disappearing from the radar?" Tammy continued to hold the wheel tight as she strained her eyes in the darkness, fearing she may hit a boat at any moment. Another dot appearing on the radar caught her attention. "Not again!" she hollered in frustration. Then again it too, disappeared. "This is not making any sense. I have to wake up Dwayne." She yelled out his name. "Dwayne! Wake up!" but he couldn't hear her over the loud noise of the engines. "Damn it," she hissed, and then saw another dot appear, then just as quickly disappear. Tammy looked hard all around her. "I don't see anything! Why are boats showing up on the radar? Dwayne!" she yelled again, but it was hopeless, he hadn't heard her.

Tammy reluctantly left the wheel and stuck her head inside the cabin, "Dwayne, wake up! I need you."

To her relief, Dwayne instantly woke up, "What's going on?" he called, sitting up, alarmed by her tone of voice.

"Get up here, I need you! There are tons of boats out here, but I don't see them. Hurry up!"

Dwayne's jaw dropped. "Oh shit! I'll be right there."

Tammy quickly returned to the helm, just in time to see another dot show up on the radar. "What are these? Friggin' ghost ships?"

Dwayne was by her side within seconds. "Where are the boats?"

Tammy pointed to the radar. "Dots keep showing up on the screen, but then they disappear. I keep looking, but I'm not seeing any boats nearby. This is really weird, I'm freaking out."

Dwayne looked at the radar screen. "I don't see anything, Tammy."

"Just wait. Keep watching the screen." Suddenly another dot appeared. "See? There's one. Now keep watching it." A few seconds later it disappeared just like the other ones. "See? I told you. It just went away. I'm telling you, there are no boats near us. I've been looking."

Dwayne looked up at the skies and then straight ahead. "How far out are we from the Marina?"

"About two miles," Tammy replied.

Dwayne chuckled and Tammy took offense. "Why are you laughing? It's not funny. There may be a bunch of boats right outside the harbor."

Dwayne chuckled again. "They're not boats, Tammy."

Tammy creased her brow. "What do you mean they're not boats? What else would show up on the radar? That piece of equipment is there to warn us of nearby vessels. It's not going to pick up cars. We're on the damn ocean."

"That's true Tammy, but it *will* pick up airplanes."

"Huh? Now why the hell would it do that?"

Dwayne pointed to the sky, "look over there and watch."

Tammy took one hand off the helm and looked out. A few seconds later she saw the lights of a plane taking off. "There goes a plane."

"Now, look at the radar screen."

Tammy turned her head and looked at the screen. "There's another dot."

"That's the plane you're looking at. LAX airport is right over there, and what the radar is picking up is the planes taking off. They take off over the ocean, and when it gets out of reach of the radar the dot disappears."

"Are you kidding me? Those are planes popping up on the screen?"

"Yep. We've got nothing to worry about."

"Well, you never told me that this thing detects planes. There needs to be a warning on this damn thing. *Not everything is a boat!*"

Dwayne laughed. "I never thought about it. We don't do too many night crossings, which is the only time we use the radar, and when we do, I normally drive us into the harbor."

"Well, I feel stupid. I honestly thought I was going to ram into a bunch of boats. Is there anything else I need to know about this thing? Does it detect sea monsters too?!"

Dwayne leaned in and embraced her. "Not yet, but I promise I'll let you know when they do!"

ACKNOWLEDGMENTS

While writing this book, Gordon and I struggled to come up with a title, so we thought we would ask our readers.

Tina has a reader's Facebook group with almost 4000 members, called *Read More Books* and asked her members for suggestions. From the many great ideas, we narrowed it down to 10 and posted a poll in the group, asking readers to vote on their favorite title.

Waves And Memories was the ultimate winner with two thirds of the votes and was suggested by *Barbara Miller*, so we wanted to give her a huge thank you for suggesting the perfect title. She will be receiving a signed copy.

ABOUT THE AUTHORS

Award winning author, Tina Hogan Grant loves to write stories with strong female characters that know what they want and aren't afraid to chase their dreams. She loves to write sexy, and

sometimes steamy romances with happy-ever after endings.

She lives life to the fullest in a small mountain community in Southern California with her husband and two dogs. When she is not writing she's probably riding her ATV, kayaking or hiking with her best friend – her husband of thirty years.

www.tinahogangrant.com

Gordon Grant lives in California and loves the great outdoors. He resides in a small mountain community in his dream home that he and his wife, Tina built together.

For over twenty years he made his living as a commercial fisherman on the Pacific Ocean and is now a professional falconer. He enjoys fishing, hunting, camping, boating, archery, and riding motorcycles.

ALSO BY TINA HOGAN GRANT

THE TAMMY MELLOWS SERIES

First Fall - Prequel

Reckless Beginnings - Book 1

Better Endings - Book 2

The Reunions Books 3

THE SABELA SERIES

Davin - Prequel

Slater - Book 1

Eve - Book 2

Claire - Book 3

Jill - Book 4

All Of Us - Book 5

Vegas Bound - Book 6

Open Arms - Book 7